The FINAL ROSE

D1569882

Amy ♡
Oliveira ?.

The Final Rose

© 2024 by Amy Oliveira

Editing by The Fiction Fix

Proofreading by Connie Gonzalez

First Edition September 2024

Cover Art and Design by Audrey Lellouche (@audreylelloucheillustration)

Probably Smut Special Edition 2025

To all of you silly enough to believe
In a meet-cute
In the perfect kiss
In romance books.

It's okay.
I believe it too.

Content Warning

The following program contains graphic sexual scenes and foul language. Viewer discretion is advised.

CHAPTER 1
Callie

Who will the famished viewers devour this year? And which women will be dumb enough to sacrifice themselves in the name of love?

Lost in my thoughts, I tap my nails against the ceramic mug. It reads *Sosa Knows Best*, a present from a cameraman last Christmas, and it's my absolute favorite vessel for my coffee.

I breathe in the fresh air of a new season all around me, and I can't stop the sly grin growing on my lips.

I *love* my job.

When Jeff took over as the director in season five, we changed our location permanently to this mansion—a ten-acre piece of real estate you can even rent off-season if you can afford the ridiculous price tag.

I leave the kitchen and sip my coffee. They hired my favorite caterers again after last year's disaster with another company. I practically lobbied to get them back here, and I'm relieved it worked. It's the best coffee in town, and I should know—I'm Colombian.

When I step outside, I'm overwhelmed by our mess. The

crew is everywhere, shouting and demanding. Gary and Troy fix the front lights, and Tiff screams about the red carpet. I should hustle. It's seven in the morning and, like every day in the entertainment business, we're running late.

"Sosa, get your ass over here!" With a hand on my brow to protect my eyes from the sun, I glance up just in time to catch Anya barking from the balcony, her red hair cascading over her shoulders.

"Sure thing, boss!" I yell back, but she already turned away.

Being careful with my hot coffee, I trail through the main house and up the stairs to the left, where only crew is allowed. I open the door and find them all there.

Anya stands with a snarl, and Jeff, a smile. Then there's Devi, Jeff's assistant, Vanessa the casting director, and the big guy, the showrunner himself, Adam Cork.

I glance over at Nessa, who jumps from one foot to the other, shaking her pigtails as she does. They've been keeping it all under wraps this season, so I know nothing about the casting. Nessa came over the other night for a face mask, boxed wine, and B-rated movies sleepover in my cramped apartment. I thought she was going to spill the beans, but no. Adam made her promise to keep it quiet.

Adam tugs at one of Vanessa's pigtails affectionately. "Calm down. You can tell her now."

Those two are fucking, *for sure*. Nessa had never said it with words, but I'm not dumb. I actually wish they would hide it *better*.

Anya's grimace amps up with that little tug on Nessa's pigtails. She disapproves of work relationships. Honestly, Anya disapproves of everything that isn't unwavering work devotion, but no one is asking her opinion, much less Adam-fucking-Cork, so she's forced to keep it to herself.

I smile at my friend. "I'm here now."

Vanessa walks toward me. "I wanted to tell you, but you know..." She glances back at them with a pout. "I told them you can keep a secret."

"It wasn't about Callie," Jeff interrupts. "You know this, Nessa."

She opens her mouth to argue again, but I interrupt before she gets too far. "Tell me already, then!"

It's a waste of time trying to argue my way into the inner circle. I have enough on my plate as it is—more than just a field producer should have, anyway.

Vanessa takes my hand and tugs me to the back of the room, where I can see the whiteboard with a sheet of paper glued to the middle. A few scribbles are dotted on the side, sticky notes with ideas and other things that definitely came from Diego and Sonja, our senior writers. I'd recognize their handwriting anywhere.

I look at the paper and raise an eyebrow at Nessa. I'm glad she works in showbiz, because my girl is dramatic. She holds my shoulders and stops me there, instructing me to stay put. Adam chuckles, but Nessa doesn't care about him. She backs up to the whiteboard and pinches the top of the white sheet, lifting it up just a little to show me she's ready for the big reveal.

"This year's most eligible bachelor..." she starts, and Adam fakes drums tapping on the table's surface. Nessa sends him a sweet smile. I laugh, which only causes Anya to roll her eyes. "The heartthrob who will soon be the wet dream of millions. The man who will pick and choose between the country's most beautiful women is..."

Adam's drumming intensifies. With a flourish, Nessa uncovers the picture, and the paper flows down, revealing the photo underneath.

Piercing blue eyes stare back at me over a star's smile and

perfectly tossed light brown hair. Under the most gorgeous headshot I've ever seen is his name in black ink.

Sebastian Riggs.

My eyes grow big.

"Sebastian Riggs?" I choke, still holding my mug. I almost strangle it.

"Oh yes, baby!" Nessa is clearly proud of herself.

I blink slowly at the man in the picture and shake my head. "He's the closest you can get to British Royalty."

That's true. I have no other words when I turn to Nessa to find she's jumping up and down.

"Can you imagine that accent on screen? It will melt panties all over the world!"

Adam clears his throat. Nessa winces and mouths an apology. They *definitely* need to hide it better.

I reach for Sebastian's picture, taking it off the board, tape on the back and all. "How the hell can we make him swear on TV?"

My tone breaks the big smile off Nessa's lips. I'm not trying to destroy her big reveal. Getting someone like Sebastian Riggs on our show is a tremendous accomplishment. Everyone always wonders if reality TV is for real, especially the dating kind. Even though we have eleven seasons behind us, and multiple couples are still together with multiple children, there are skeptics out there.

Sure, finding love on a TV show is unconventional, but so is online dating, and last year alone, I went to three weddings from people who swiped right. Sebastian Riggs as our Eligible is a huge tick in our pro column.

I can't believe the picture in my hands. The Englishman is a CEO, a philanthropist, and easily the most desired bachelor in the world. He's serious and respected, and it's a game-changer to have him bring that kind of credibility to *The Final Rose*. But still—*still*—we're making a reality show here, and there's no way someone as distinguished as Sebastian Riggs would bring the kind of drama people expect.

"I have a plan, kid." I swear, Anya can read my thoughts.

"Sebastian will bring a lot of publicity," Nessa insists, chewing on her bottom lip. I feel bad my reaction wasn't jumping up and down like she clearly envisioned.

"I'm sure." I smile brightly, trying to reassure her. "This is huge, Nessa."

A calming sigh escapes her, and I feel more like an asshole than ever.

"I'm just worrying he's not a potty mouth like the rest of our singles." I smirk. "But I heard British TV can be a shit-show just like ours, right?"

Jeff chuckles. "Not everything is *The Great British Baking Show*, no."

"Yeah, I'm worrying about nothing," I tell Nessa.

"Oh, no, you keep on worrying," Anya interrupts. "We have goody two shoes over there." She nods at the picture of Sebastian I'm holding. "But we have twelve ladies coming, and they are not even a little like royalty."

I smile at Anya. She's a tough nut to crack, but I like her style. It's hard to find someone like her to mentor you, a hard ass and a good boss at the same time.

"What else do you have, Nessa?"

My friend beams at me and grabs a tablet resting on the table. For the next hour, I'm given a crash course on the twelve women who hope to make Sebastian Riggs fall in love.

CHAPTER 2
Sebastian

"You're mad."

My oldest friend chuckles from the other side of the line and the ocean. Maverick can't see why I would ever be part of a reality TV show, especially the dating kind. I relax my shoulders on the sea of pillows in the hotel provided by the network, one hand holding the phone and the other arm supporting my head.

"I'll be fine."

He frowns. "You're going to be on the telly, Sebastian."

I shrug. "I'm on TV all the time."

Maverick puffs. He knows I'm downplaying it. Taking a picture here or there and giving a statement after a charity ball is very different from putting myself out there like this. "Don't worry about me."

"Hard not to when I'm sure you hit your noggin. I'm on the edge of my seat here, mate. I'm just waiting until you lose it so we have to rescue you."

By "*we*", he means him and his husband, Fael. That would be my rescuing team—my oldest friend, his perfect husband, and their two dogs. I love them, but their annoying happiness is one of the reasons I accepted the offer to be on *The Final Rose*. But I don't say that to Maverick. I won't hear the end of it if I tell him I hope to find someone who will move in with me to the neighboring house so we can raise our poodles side by side. I don't say it because then he'll know for sure I've lost my mind.

"My contract is ironclad," I assure him one more time. "No nudity, no lies, no outlandish plots to see how I'll react on TV."

"They have to make it entertaining. They will pull something."

I know he's right. I watched enough seasons of *The Final Rose* to know there's always drama. I'm signing up for months of dating multiple women in front of the cameras. I know there will be drama. I just won't accept *created* drama.

"I know how to mind myself." I nod to no one. "The contract also helps."

Maverick laughs, and I'm not sure if I'll ever convince him it's a good idea, but I'm ready to move on. A town car will take me to the mansion tomorrow morning, and I'm a little nervous.

"What do your parents think of *The Final Rose*?"

I swear under my breath. I prefer to talk about how the producers will trick me into doing something unseemly on camera rather than about what the Riggses think of their son on reality TV.

They don't think highly of it, no. I might seem like a good egg, but my mother and father have been disagreeing with my choices for a long time now. I chose the wrong university, girl-friends from the wrong circles, the wrong accountant for my business, the wrong secretary for my office. Nothing is good enough for them, so it got to the point where I stopped caring.

What can be done when they simply insist on being pompous fucks?

"They've never watched it," I confess.

"I can only imagine their faces at watching the terror unfolding in front of their eyes as you drag the Riggs' good name through the mud."

"Well, I'm doing it anyway. I signed a contract with the network before telling them, but Mum's still calling me non-stop. She's trying to get me back to London. I'm supposed to see reason, you see."

"Well, now I want you to stay and be brilliant on TV." He changes his mind. "Indecorous, if you will. Anything to upset Mummy Riggs. You know where I stand."

I laugh because, of course, Maverick would prefer to die before standing on the side as good English society. I guess I've got him on board finally, and it's all I could ask for.

"You're starting with makeup, and then you'll wait for Callie there."

I have to jog to follow the woman. It's not even seven in the morning, and everything on the set seems to be in full swing. Dozens of people move about the front garden, all in black shirts with *The Final Rose* logos in the upper left-hand corner.

I do not know who the woman beside me is, but she walks fast and talks even faster. I didn't get a good morning or an introduction when I arrived. The car door opened as soon as we parked, and she has been talking ever since.

We navigate the halls, my palms sweaty with nerves, and for the first time, it dawns on me that I'm set to be on television. I'm in Los Angeles, and I agreed to be on a reality TV show to find love.

Maybe my parents were right to be absolutely disgusted.

I gulp and try not to look like I'm about to bolt, following the woman's steps until we reach a bigger room to the right of the mansion. It smells like strong perfume and the hairspray mother uses when she's going to a charity event. A woman no older than eighteen with green hair and multiple facial piercings waits by a chair. She turns to me when we arrive, her eyes cataloging my form like she's making a list of things that need to be corrected.

"I'll send Callie," the woman barks at the makeup artist and turns on her heels.

"Thank you?" I say. Her intimidating demeanor makes me question myself, and when I turn, the makeup artist has a little smile.

"Forgive Anya. She's not really a people person." She gestures to her makeup chair, and I sit.

"Oh, I thought she was terribly polite."

She snorts, clicking her tongue. "They're going to put up a sign every time you talk."

"Do I need subtitles?"

"For your sarcasm." She arches a brow, looking at me through the mirror. "I'm Doris, by the way."

Doris—what an old-fashioned name for a young girl with green hair. "I'm Sebastian. Tell me this will be quick."

Doris tilts her head to the side. Bringing her finger to my chin, she turns my head from one side to the other.

"You're looking clammy and red."

"Terrific."

"It won't take long." She ignores me. "I'll do something about your hair, too." She picks up a strand, feeling the quality of it.

Now I feel like a horse waiting to know its value—I'm not very valuable, if I'm going by Doris' face.

I'm told I have a head full of hair, like that's the best news she can give me. Then, I'm taken to the sink to get my hair washed while Doris tells me all about how things could be much worse. By the end of my washing, I'm indeed glad that all I am is clammy and red-faced.

We are back in the chair. Doris has a hair dryer on hand, its wire looping around her neck as she selects the best-looking brush from her cart.

"I'm sorry I'm late, Doris!" says an unfamiliar voice. "You know how it is..."

My gaze locks onto the new stranger through the mirror. She's wearing the same branded shirt as the rest of the crew. Her shoulder-length, wavy hair is partially down, the top part twisted in a bun, denim shorts and old-looking trainers rounding out her look. She has a walkie-talkie hooked to the waistband of her shorts and a clipboard in hand.

This must be Callie, the one I was promised.

We regard each other through the mirror. Her eyes are warm, her bottom lip full. They told me American girls were good-looking, but Callie is something else.

"You must be Sebastian. I'm sorry I'm late." She moves from behind me, grabbing a chair to the side and turning it so we can look at each other while Doris works her magic.

The hair dryer muffles Callie's next words.

"What?" I ask over the noise.

"I'm Callie!" she says louder, throwing Doris a look. "I'm going to wait..." She shakes her head, annoyed at shouting to be heard.

Doris turns off the hair dryer. "I'm doing my job, Sosa."

"Do it quietly," Callie replies with warmth. "It's not even seven in the morning."

"Well, maybe it's good for you to exercise that voice and..."

Callie narrows her eyes. "Are you in on the bet?"

Doris doesn't reply and turns on the thing again. Callie sighs, turns around, and takes the wire off the plug.

"Hey!"

"I can't believe you're in on the bet!" Callie accuses.

I shake my head, trying to follow. "What bet?"

I half expect them to keep talking over me, but Callie actually replies. "They have a bet on how long it will take for me to lose my voice. It took a month last season and a month and a half the season before."

"Is she a screamer?" I ask Doris.

She chuckles. "Oh, I like the way he says it. You'll do great on television."

I give a flashy grin. "Brilliant. It's my lifelong dream."

Callie chews on her lip. "He's gonna need a sarcasm sign or something."

"I know!" Doris agrees over my head.

CHAPTER 3
Callie

"Today, we'll go easy. For the initial interview, we're going with your thoughts and hopes for the show and your first impressions of the mansion." I look down at my schedule and keep talking. "And then we have a break for lunch..."

"Pardon?" he asks, bringing my attention back to his face.

Okay, yes, so maybe I'm avoiding looking directly at Sebastian Riggs. He's so handsome, it should be illegal. It's wild to admit it when I've been with the show for years; I've seen some pretty people. I live in Los Angeles, for God's sake!

It's honestly the opposite of what people might think—working with pretty people makes me care less about my appearance. I meet so many gorgeous, breathtaking women that now I know I can't compete. So, I don't even try.

I put on mascara each day because I like my eyelashes long, but that's it, other than the obligatory sunscreen. And then, of course, there are my clothes.

I have about ten branded t-shirts from the show, and while I could wear anything and no one would give a crap, I like not having to think of an outfit in the morning. I'm always wearing shorts, except for that one chilly week of the year when my ten-year-old pair of jeans are required.

All in all, beauty doesn't register anymore; the lack of mine, nor the abundance of other's.

Sebastian Riggs shakes that resolve a little.

It's the accent, I decide. It has nothing to do with his intense, water-blue eyes, perfectly shaped mouth, or lustrous hair. God, he's got me calling his hair *lustrous*! But no, I'm certain it's the accent that makes him more appealing than your average L.A. boy-toy.

When I look up, his goddamn intense gaze is pinned on me. *Oh, here we go.*

"What part of the schedule didn't you get?" I ask, confused. Honestly; I dumbed this down for him.

"Are you asking for my first impressions and then it's lunchtime?"

"Hmm, yes. That's correct."

He glances at his watch. "How long will the interview take?"

Doris snickers behind him, and I nod, understanding. He's assuming I'm going to ask a couple of questions, and we all can go on our merry way. Nothing is ever that simple when you're changing camera angles.

"Everything takes time," I say, trying to be conciliatory. I don't want to scare him too quickly. "Don't worry too much about the schedule."

"I wouldn't dream of it," he replies, and I almost miss the glint in his eyes. He has a good sense of humor, and I have to bite my cheek to not chuckle with him.

"You have to tone that down."

"Tone what down?" He clamps his mouth closed when Doris brushes his hair and sprays a generous amount of product into it with no notice.

"You're kinda bitchy."

Sebastian flashes me a look.

"You're a little snarky. Sounds like you don't want to be here."

He considers that. "I want to be here. I'm just having a laugh."

This time, I don't hold the chuckle back. "Did you have media training?"

He scoffs. "Naturally."

He's so...different from everyone else here. One second, he's sarcastic and unruly, and the next, he talks like he's Mr. Darcy himself. It's mind-boggling and not hot at all. *No, sir, an English dude with a sarcastic streak is the opposite of hot.*

"Well, I'm going to give you a few tips for free anyway," I say, and I am not discouraged when he rolls his eyes. "The lenses take you at face value."

"Pardon?"

I hold my chuckle. "People out there will buy what you show. They don't read between the lines; they don't give you the benefit of the doubt. They aren't interested in your tone. If you complain about the show, they will assume you don't want to be here. If you make fun of the girls, they will make you the bad guy." To this, his mouth closes in a flat line. "If you talk like a royal, they will think you're Prince Charming."

He huffs. "And am I correct to assume that's the face you'd like me to show?"

"Yes. I'd love to have Prince Charming falling in love on TV, but I want you to be real too..."

"Because drama brings ratings."

I sigh. He's nothing like I thought he was going to be. I put my clipboard to the side, crossing my arms over my chest. When I heard about Sebastian Riggs for the first time, I thought he was going to be too much of a gentleman to be entertaining. I thought we wouldn't have any story to show. What kind of character arc is one supposed to construct when he's perfect already? But now, I see a different angle altogether.

"What kind of media training were you given?"

Sebastian rolls his shoulders back. "I know how to behave at a dinner, how to be discreet in a busy restaurant. But I'm not used to watching my mouth all the time."

"So, you're picture perfect, not camera ready?" I arch an eyebrow.

"Sure."

My lips twitch. "Why are you here, Sebastian?"

"Pardon?" he asks for the third time, and I realize it's a crutch. It's the polite word he says to avoid asking people to shut their mouths.

"You heard me. Why did you decide to be part of our show?"

Doris finishes with his hair right in time, glancing at me before stepping back to get the makeup cart. I'm left watching Sebastian, waiting for a sarcastic reply. He flashes me a look and says, "I want to find someone."

This takes me by surprise. "Do you?"

He shrugs, turning to the mirror and avoiding my eyes. "I like the idea of settling down. And whatever way I'd try to meet someone would be unconventional anyway."

"Why do you think so?"

"Because I'm a bloody Riggs, aren't I?"

"Tell me what that means," I ask, and it's not because I'm being nosy. Suddenly, I really want to understand how we managed to get someone like Sebastian on our show. It's more than publicity with him, I can tell.

"I thought you wanted to keep the messy parts to show on camera."

"Maybe I need a taste–" I correct myself immediately, "A warning! So we know what to expect, of course."

"The women back home already know my name. I can't

be on a dating app. I can't meet someone at the gym like normal people. When I go on dates, it's with friends of friends, or worse, friends of the family. It's all very...stiff and arranged. So why not? It doesn't matter at this point. We won't have a meet-cute walking in the park with our dogs—"

"You're looking for the plot of *101 Dalmatians* in your future wife?"

He doesn't even entertain my question. "I'm happy to be here. My apologies if I gave you the wrong impression."

I click my tongue, tilting my head to the side. It's like I have three versions of the same man. One has a dry humor that won't necessarily translate well on camera. The other is distant and way too proper. But this new one right here? This one is for real.

To make it on TV, you need to connect with people, and you can only do that if you're vulnerable. His handsome face will get him through a couple of episodes, but soon, the audience will want something else. They want to watch a show about an English aristocrat to see him fall in love with a peasant.

People want to keep the fairytale alive.

Doris comes back with the makeup cart, starting with his skin, and I watch them for a second, my head running a mile a minute.

"Be Prince Charming for me," I finally say. "Let me sell that, and I'll get your princess."

Sebastian turns his gaze toward me and gives the most minuscule nod.

We have a deal.

"What do you think?"

The mansion is too busy, so we're in Anya's trailer, which is actually the production's trailer, but it's a pit because Anya doesn't believe in picking up after herself.

"He's the same as all of them," she grunts.

I sip my coffee and smile at her. Sebastian is nothing like any contestant I've ever seen.

"Tell me you got something on him."

I lift one shoulder. "He talks like a dream. It will melt panties. Nessa is right."

Another grunt. "Who cares? Are you filming thirteen episodes of him reading line cards to the cameras? Don't be stupid."

I honestly think people would turn their TV on just to hear Sebastian read a grocery list, but I don't say that.

"You told me you had a plan." I poke her, nudging her to the whiteboard, where she has pinned a picture of all the contestants set to arrive tomorrow.

"Depends on what you have for me." She crosses her arms and cracks a smile.

I'm not sure what to say to her. Sebastian seemed sincere, but I'll sound dumb if I tell my boss a grown man is truly trying to find the love of his life on television. Of course, no one says straight away that they're only here for publicity; they all spin lies about love. But they're usually accompanied by their publicist nudging their arms before they let any truth escape their lips.

Riggs looked dead into my eyes and said he had the best of intentions.

I feel naïve to even consider he's telling the truth, but there was no one whispering in his ear, and he doesn't seem like the type looking for publicity at all costs.

The words are stuck in my mouth. One of us is gullible.

Maybe it's Sebastian for believing in love, or maybe it's me for believing in him.

"He has a mild personality and tries to be kind," I tell her, leaving any comments about his dry humor unsaid.

Anya nods, looking over the board with a hand to her chin, lost in thought.

"A wild child?" she considers, pointing to the picture of a particular busty redhead.

I shake my head. "She'll eat him alive. People might dislike her."

"Good." Anya nods. "We need a villain too."

"He needs someone kind," I start before she suggests something more. "Maybe someone shy and..."

"A kindergarten teacher." She pokes the picture of a smiley brunette.

I try to imagine Sebastian and the woman together, but something is missing. A spark? She looks too boring, too normal for someone like him. He needs a spine too.

My eyes wander, reading their names and professions below each picture. Nessa told us more about them before, but I forgot already. My eyes stop on a beautiful woman with an assertive smile. She's a scientist.

"What about her?" I ask. "She's smart, maybe a little nerdy?"

Anya considers her. "Ask Vanessa to bring her video interview. I want to see her on camera before committing."

"We need to see her chemistry with Sebastian before..."

Anya waves me off, clearly not interested in what Sebastian might think. Usually, the contestants are easily steered in the right direction. They are all good-looking women. What's there to complain about? But something tells me Sebastian would not like to be steered.

I can't tell her that, though. Anya has been with *The Final*

Rose since season two when the show really blew up. She has architected nine relationships, six of them lasting at least six months after the show finished. At this point, Anya has a God complex and very little patience. I have more self-preservation than telling her Sebastian is different only based on a gut feeling.

We only watch the video once Nessa, Sonja, and Diego join us. Nessa has all the answers we need. Her kind nature makes her connect with people quickly, and they always spill their secrets.

Nessa already knows who is here for love, who is clever, and who's naïve. She knows what might work with each personality type, a gift that goes beyond her profession. Our writers sit and absorb everything, taking notes and thinking on a course of action.

It's *reality* TV. It doesn't matter how much we move and poke; if the Eligible doesn't like the contestant, he will eliminate her regardless of what kind of storyline we're plotting. While Anya, Diego, and Sonja see it as a job, stacking blocks as they see fit, scripting lines like we're all part of a play, I know Nessa sees it like I do.

This is matchmaking.

Sure, I'm not *that* romantic, but I know deep in my heart, feelings can't be influenced.

Sebastian needs to come out of this happy. Only then is the audience going to be happy. And if the audience is happy, the network is too.

We are here only to nudge. I never showed the camera a lie, never put words in someone's mouth. Everything portrayed on screen is true. You can't make someone say something.

And even though I know all of that, when Diego is drafting a script, my stomach churns.

"Vera is the best angle." Diego nods. "She's smart, caring, and shy."

"We keep Kirsten as a backup." Sonja nods. "She's good too. Doesn't pack a punch like Vera, but…" She shrugs. "Maybe Riggs is a secret jerk, and Vera looks too smart to put up with that."

I feel the urge to defend Sebastian, but I hold my tongue just in time.

I'm a single, young Latina working in the entertainment business. I have the best asshole radar in town, and Sebastian? He's not one of them.

I know Anya trusts my instincts. That's why she sends me to meet the Eligible first. I usually come back with plenty of information, and we plan the season in between laughs.

This time around, though, I'm barely talking.

I have a good feeling about Sebastian, but for some reason, I prefer to keep it to myself. I let them plan his life for the next three months. I hear the good and bad of each contestant and try to hold back comments. But at the end of the meeting, Anya watches me with a wariness that pricks at my skin.

CHAPTER 4
Sebastian

"Are you nervous?"

"I'm not nervous."

"Don't make that face, then."

"What face?"

I turn just in time to see Callie bugging her eyes out and quivering her lips. I scoff, standing tall in the front garden. Cameramen are coming from all sides, a thick red carpet laid from the front door to the sidewalk. In the second I take to react to her taunting, Callie's attention is back to the walkie-talkie, barking orders. She's in her usual uniform: denim shorts, *The Final Rose* tee, and battered trainers. Her head barely comes up to my shoulders, and I suppress the urge to pet her or something. I hardly think she would appreciate that.

She talks fast and curses in Spanish now and again to whoever is in the vicinity. The next stream coming out of her mouth is especially colorful, and I have to bite back a laugh.

"You speak Spanish?" she asks.

"A much tamer version of it, but yes."

"Of course." She rolls her eyes. "Well, pretend you don't, *cabrón*."

This time, I flash her a smile I know has worked with many women. Maverick has running bits about the smile I give to people, but to my utter disappointment, Callie just frowns and turns away.

She's now shouting at other men who aren't me. Honestly, watching is much better than being the recipient.

It doesn't take long to notice Callie thinks everyone does everything wrong but her. There she goes, from one point of the garden to the other, quick on her feet, fixing the whole set.

Finally, she's back to my side, fixing me and my tie.

"I know how to keep a tie straight," I say, but I only get a little smirk from her.

"The first car is five minutes from here," she tells me.

I look around for just a second, and it's clear we're ready to go. The madness that was here just a second ago disappeared like magic. Everyone is back in place and the cameras are rolling. The crew holds their breath, and I wonder if I should hold mine too.

I swallow and try to hide my real feelings. I *am* nervous, but anyone would be if they were waiting to meet their future wife.

"Tell me about her."

"Mystery is romantic," Callie argues.

"Give me one word." I flash the smile again, the one that doesn't work with her.

"One word about the girl? Just one?" she checks, and I dip my chin.

Someone calls for Callie's attention. A car stops at the corner and waits for the signal. She steps back, and I'm sure my request will be ignored. But at the last minute, she whispers, "Southern belle."

I meet Grace, the southern belle. Isla, the yoga instructor. Kirsten, the kindergarten teacher. I'm pleasant and try my best to engage and give them dashing smiles, but the truth is, I'm dizzy.

Each time a car rolls forward, a woman in a gorgeous gown emerges, and the camera gets us at a good angle. I barely have time to say hello before she goes inside, just so I can do it all again.

Their faces merge. I remember some, a couple of names, but nothing grabs my attention besides Callie's insights.

After Grace, I asked her once more for a tip as the second girl prepared to arrive. That's when she said, "Vegan", and then I met Abby.

My memory is betraying me. I wish I had Maverick here. He's great with faces and names. That's why he has always been the perfect companion to social functions, even though Mum hates it—thinks the press will assume I'm gay and interfere with her chances of finding me a proper match.

Maverick is a brilliant talker, a real people person. It's easy to make conversation with him by my side, but now that I'm alone, I appreciate his talents even more.

Sweat covers my forehead, though the makeup crew keeps fussing over me. Nothing can hide that I stood under the sun in a suit for far too long.

I'm loosening up my tie when a huge bouquet approaches my face. I grab it on instinct, and Callie appears behind it.

"What's this?"

She shrugs. "It came for you. You're supposed to fall in love *here*, you know? You can't have a shorty on the side."

"Funny," I reply and open the small envelope on top of the wildflowers.

What a star! I bet the whole lot fancies you after that dashing smile.
-Maverick

I throw my head back and laugh. Of course, Maverick would find a way to send something. I look at the flowers and recognize his taste, something sophisticated and wild at the same time. I'm still smiling at the card when a tiny hand comes to my arm and pinches—*hard*.

"Oi!"

"You don't have a girlfriend or something, right?" she demands.

"What woman sends flowers to her boyfriend?" I ask, amused if anything.

"And do I know English dating rules?"

My lips curl into a smile. It's easy to feel comfortable around Callie. That must be why she's so successful at her job. Besides the rod up her arse when the cameras are rolling, she's otherwise easygoing and friendly. We've only known each other for a couple of days, and she's already comfortable enough to hurt me.

"It's from my friend Maverick," I tell her, showing the card. "He likes to cause a commotion."

Her eyes dart quickly to the words on the card, and then she looks at me. "So, the girls are supposed to *fancy* you," she says like it's a made-up word. I hold my laugh back again. "Because of your smile?"

"It's proven to be effective."

Callie's hand goes to her waist as she watches me under an

arched brow. Around us, the crew takes everything apart. The next segment is inside the mansion, where I'm supposed to say a few words to the girls and welcome them to their new home.

I should fix myself so I don't look absolutely ghastly, but I'm here instead, looking at Callie's perfectly symmetrical face and those daring brown eyes.

"Give it to me," she says, curling her finger in a *come-at-me* motion.

"What?"

"Give me your best smile. The one your friend thinks can melt panties."

I chuckle, trying to buy time. I know damn well it doesn't work with her, but I say nothing. I simply shake my head. "It's my normal smile. Maverick is just—"

"But you said it was effective."

"I was joking."

"Just show me!" I have the feeling she won't let this go.

"Why do you want to see me smile so badly?" I challenge her.

"Because you're on TV, and if your smile can melt panties..."

"I never said it can melt panties," I argue. "That's speculation."

"Smile."

"Not on command."

"You're infuriating."

"Don't tell that to the audience."

Our back and forth is so quick, I know no one would follow. I feel alive under my skin, my fingers tingling as I try hard not to open a beaming smile for the woman in front of me. Her eyes dart across my face. Her mouth curves just a little, but quickly, she bites her lip and puts a stop to it.

"Sosa, are you done here? Anya wants you inside," a crew member calls.

Callie's eyes are still on me as she replies. "Yep, I'm done here." She turns on her heels and says, to no one and everyone, "Someone fix Riggs. He looks like soggy toilet paper."

This time, I can't hold it. I throw my head back and laugh.

I'm not sure if it's procedure or not, but I get a little file with all the girls' names, photos, and bios. Nothing much to go on, just enough for me to memorize each face and make a brief association of what I was told today.

I look at the pictures from Abby to Vivian, trying to find a spark, a miracle, but nothing happens. I feel stupid. Of course, I wasn't expecting to fall in love at first sight, but I wished to at least have a vivid memory of the girls. Besides the fact that they are all absolutely gorgeous, nothing comes to mind.

And I have to eliminate one.

That's when I ring Maverick, with no concern about what time it is in London. As he answers, groaning over the phone, I know I called at a bad time. But I don't ask, I just say:

"I have to eliminate one of them."

"Already?" His voice sounds thick with sleep.

"Yes."

"Eliminate the one you care for the least." He says it like it's simple.

"I know nothing about them." I sigh, frustrated. "I met them for a second one-on-one as they arrived, and then we had a quick drink."

"But no one stood out?"

I place the photos on my bed, looking from one woman to the next. I'm already shaking my head.

"We talked as a group. They were funny and nice, but it's not like I had the opportunity to really meet them."

"So be shallow," my oldest friend suggests. "Eliminate the one you think is the least attractive."

I tsk. "They are all supermodel kind of hot."

Maverick hums on the other side of the ocean. "Ok, let's do this at three in the morning. Tell me, is there anything that calls to you first in a woman?"

Without meaning to, I think of the producer, Callie. From the second I laid my eyes on her, I couldn't forget her face. It's not just her beauty, but the mischief in her eyes, the sharp words coming from her mouth.

"I like attitude," I tell him. "But it's hard to know who has it when I've barely met them. It's unfair."

"Seb, just..." I can envision him rubbing his face, annoyed. "Tell me about one of them you remember."

I chase it in my mind without looking at their pictures. I smile because the one who comes to mind is Grace, the southern belle. Callie said I made the most ridiculous face when she gave me the tip about the contestant. I didn't know what to expect of a southern belle.

"Grace."

"Good, good. So, she stays. Next?"

I chase the thread, and then I think of Summer, who Callie described as *long legs.* One by one, I tell Maverick as I remember them, trying to connect names and faces. I'm running out of names when I get to ten.

"So, who is left?"

I take two pictures, Vera and Elliana. I can't really remember either of them, and I try my hardest to picture the moment they arrived or what Callie said, but I can't.

"I don't remember them at all."

"Well, so it's one of them you have to eliminate."

I look down at their pictures. Besides that, I only have

their age and where they're from. There isn't much to go on. For all I know, one of these girls might be the love of my life, but unfortunately, she only had thirty seconds to make an impression.

"And who is Callie?"

I'm so absorbed in the pictures, I almost miss what he's asking.

"Hmm?"

"Who's Callie?"

"Why are you asking?" I put the pictures aside.

"Nothing," he replies in that way of his that means it's everything. "Just the name I heard the most."

I relax a little, rolling my eyes. "Callie is a field producer, and she was helping me memorize each girl."

"How?"

I chuckle, sitting on the bed with my back to the headboard. "She'd say just one or two words before every girl arrived."

"Almost like a game?"

"I guess." I chuckle once more.

"So, Callie is funny," Maverick confirms.

"I guess," I say again, but I'm frowning.

"And is she young?"

I'm shaking my head before he even finishes the sentence. "Callie is the producer, not a contestant."

"Funny how your mind goes to the gutter so easily."

"You must be hallucinating. It's too early for you."

"You should really check the time before you make the call, by the way."

"I thought you wanted to be involved in this, mate. I got your flowers."

"I mean, yes, just not so early. Now tell me more about this Callie."

"Good night, Maverick."

"I'm up now, you prick."
And even though he curses, I know it's all good.

CHAPTER 5
Callie

The huge flower bouquet falls into his lap, and I cross my arms over my chest.

"If you have a girlfriend, Riggs..."

He laughs, showing off the perfect column of his neck. Taking the card, he reads it before passing it on to me.

Good luck breaking Vera's heart.
-Maverick

I read it and then read it again. I can't believe it, even as I blink at the words printed in front of my face.

The absolutely outrageous words!

Because it's impossible that he's eliminating Vera first, and even more ridiculous is that he's telling his friend and getting flowers about the spoiler.

I tear the card apart in desperation. I don't care what Riggs has to say, but he doesn't even see it. He's gone already, and I have to jog to catch up.

He passes the bouquet to a PA as he smiles at her, making the poor girl trip over her feet. I suppress a groan. That damn Englishman charm! That damn smile and the accent. I'm so angry at him, I refuse to find him charming.

"Are you eliminating Vera?" I hiss as soon as the PA is out of earshot.

He only spares me a glance.

"Are you allowed to tell me that?"

"I'm not telling you. I read about it!"

Sebastian looks from one side to the other, and I follow suit. When it's clear we're relatively alone, he lowers his voice.

"It's just Maverick."

I wiggle my finger at him. "Do you understand what can happen if anyone knows you're sharing information?"

"I'm not sharing information. I don't even have the information to share."

"This is information." I point to the general area where I was when I read the card. "It's not possible you think it's ok to do this."

He winces. "I know, I know, but I needed to talk to someone. I'm telling you, *I don't have information.*"

Sebastian says the last part like it's a code he's trying to convey. I find myself crossing my arms over my chest. "What do you mean?"

"I don't know these girls, Callie."

The way he says my name makes a chill go up my spine. I don't know if he ever said it before. I don't care about the way it makes me feel. And I hate—*hate*—the delicious sound the syllables make in his mouth.

Because I'm Callie Sosa, and I refuse to dwell on how a man pronounces my name. I force a reply through my dry mouth. "You knew the drill."

I hate myself the second the words are out. We all know the first elimination is based on appearances only. Sure, we can edit enough interactions and interviews to weave some kind of narrative, and the public will know a little about the girls and hopefully get their favorites. But the people who are here in real life?

The days are long, but they don't have time to talk organically. I know Sebastian probably can't tell the girls apart or remember all their names.

It's an overwhelming experience, and the thing is, *we want him to be overwhelmed*. This show is a game. It toys with the girls, and it toys with the Eligible.

The only reason I'm okay with it is because of what I just told him. *He knows the drill.* Each one of them is a consenting adult of sound mind who has watched many seasons of *The Final Rose* before.

Sebastian looks away from me, raking his fingers through his soft-looking hair. "I just rang Maverick to make sense of things."

I nod. It's not exactly a crime to want to talk through it with a friend, but to the network's lawyers, it's a violation of the NDA.

"I get it. But if you do it again, your ass will be sued."

He lets out a raggedy breath, and I almost pity him. "I know, I know!" His palms are up in defeat. "I'm just..."

And then, I do the unthinkable. I feel bad for the hot guy. "You can call me next time."

Sebastian's eyes raise to fix on mine, his expression as surprised as I feel when the words escape my lips.

What an idiotic suggestion.

I'm ready to back out of it when something crosses his eyes—a little twinkle. "Would you answer my call?"

"I just said that."

"It was late at night."

I groan. "How late?"

"Late. It was an ordeal." He can't hide his smirk.

"I'm regretting it now. Forget what I suggested." And to break eye contact, I resume walking.

He follows me though. "Don't think I can forget such a heartfelt offer."

"It was heartfelt. I'm helping you avoid a lawsuit. I'm probably your best friend."

"I don't doubt it. Maverick only sends me flowers. What good does that do?"

I press my step forward toward the back of the mansion. "I've been thinking about that. I don't think flowers are good for anything."

"Aren't you the most romantic? Now tell me, wouldn't your boyfriend be cross if I call preposterously late every night?"

I laugh, shaking my head. "Shameful, really."

"What?" he asks with a straight face.

"You're trying to pry into my life."

"I'm only trying not to step on anyone's toes."

"The only toe you'll step on is mine if you call *preposterously* late."

Sebastian claps his hands in animatedly. "Well, it's settled, then. I'll call you next time I need to make a decision."

I halt to a stop. A decision. Yes, the wrong decision he made about eliminating Vera, of all people.

He stops with me, a crease between his brows as he watches me chew on my lip. Everyone is betting on Vera. Just by the crew's first impression of her, she's the nicest—by far. It'll be so easy to make her the princess of this season. Beautiful, intelligent. You can't get much better than Vera.

And the fool wants to eliminate her first.

"Why Vera?" I ask.

Sebastian shrugs. "I couldn't remember anything remarkable about her."

"She has a STEM job," I hurry to say. "She cooks, she's gorgeous, and..."

"Why Vera?" He turns it around on me.

"Excuse me?"

"Why are you advocating for her? And if I told you I was between Vera and Elliana?"

I bite my tongue not to scream Elliana's name. She's nice enough, but she's not the horse we're all betting on.

"Listen, you said yourself, you know little about these girls."

"And you do?" he challenges.

"I know Vera is nice. You should wait a little. I think you'll like her."

He's still not convinced. I'm not even sure he remembers who Vera is, honestly. As a collective, they're all hot, shiny, and dressed in beautiful clothes.

But this narrative with Vera will work.

Five years ago, we would pair him with Kirsten. A kind, midwestern schoolteacher and British royalty? Perfect television. I still think she can be the runner-up, dividing the country a little. She has the charisma to pull it off.

But today, Vera is the image we need. She's a woman of color working in science. She's the role model *I* needed when I was growing up. And like Sebastian, I get the impression she's here to find love.

"I can get you a group date, right out of the gate," I bargain.

"A group date?"

"Four girls."

"Three?"

Impossible.

"I'll try, but one of them has to be Vera," I say, lowering my voice.

Usually, I'm better than this. I'm great at nudging people

in the right direction without them realizing it, but for some reason, I don't think it will work with Sebastian.

He's a man of direct words. Infuriating, really, but I can't work around him. He just asks, point blank. And now? He's asking *why Vera*.

"Do you really think I should give her a chance?"

I sigh. "Yes, I do." I'm not lying. It's not because the writers are working on the angle, or because Anya is salivating over their pairing. I actually think Sebastian would work with someone like Vera.

"Group date," he says again.

"Group date. You'll get to know them."

"All right," he agrees, and this time, when I move away, he doesn't follow.

"We have a problem," I say, flying into the producer's trailer.

Anya is always ready for trouble, so she barely bats an eyelid. Her posture is lazy against the counter. With a flick of her wrist, she tells me to keep going.

I close the door gently behind me. "He was going to eliminate Vera."

The room chills to the news. There are only a few people here, mainly those who report to Anya but are below my role. All eyes are on me as I take a seat.

"Says he doesn't know them well enough to make an informed decision."

"It's week one." Anya frowns. "Of course, he doesn't know anyone yet. Has he *ever* watched the show?"

"They usually go for appearance," one assistant, Miriam, interjects. "Maybe he doesn't think Vera is attractive."

For some reason, that bothers me. I'm probably a fool, but I really want Sebastian to be the real deal. I want to believe his words, and he said the problem was about getting to know them.

"Either way, I talked him out of it," I decide to say instead of voicing my silly beliefs.

"Who's going now?" Anya asks, a pencil between her fingers, the eraser banging against the table.

"Elliana."

They all shrug, not very concerned—which also bothers me. I've been doing this for years, but the idea of Sebastian thinking about this with care while we simply change names on a whiteboard feels...wrong.

"He needs a group date," I tell them in one breath.

"Sure, let's get the seven he calls first and..."

Anya is talking a mile a minute, but my mouth feels scratchy, and I clear my throat.

I know the show's structure. I know how it works for the first two weeks. He's *supposed* to be overwhelmed. The girls are *supposed* to fight for his attention.

"What's with the face, Callie?" Anya is not even looking at me properly. It's like she can feel it.

"Don't you think maybe it's best for a smaller group date this time?"

She turns completely my way, her eyes pinning me in place. "Why?"

Anya is a woman of a few words. She doesn't waste time beating around the bush.

Normally, I'd tell the truth. They want us to form bonds with the contestants. It's a way to know what's going to happen before it does. My job is to know, to understand, and hers is to plan accordingly.

But then, I think about Sebastian confiding in his best friend, worried about making the wrong decision.

I think of his promise to call me instead, and for no reason whatsoever, I remember when he pried into my life.

My cheeks warm, and I look down at my shoes because I don't trust Anya not to read all the unsaid words on my face.

"Vera is quiet and shy. If we want her to shine, we need to give her a less challenging setting."

It isn't a lie. Vera won't be the one talking the loudest, saying the most outrageous things to get extra camera time.

"If she doesn't shine, maybe this isn't for her." Anya insists.

"It will cause jealousy," Bay, an assistant, says at the back. "Throw them for a loop when they find out such intimate group dates are being given right from the start."

In this setting, causing jealousy is a good thing, so I build on that. "It's almost a star-crossed lovers story," I start with a little more bite. "Vera and Sebastian go perfectly together. The public falls in love with them, and then the group scenes are overwhelming, and they never get a minute alone."

"Suddenly, the whole country wants them to have a chance to be alone." Anya waggles her pencil in my direction.

"Exactly."

I tell myself it's the best solution for all sides. Sebastian has time to get to know the girls better before another elimination, Vera has time to shine, and Anya is happy with our direction.

However, shame burns underneath my skin. I don't understand where it's coming from, and I hate it. I love my job, and I have never had a problem with it.

Yes, it's a little scripted, but the couples are real. There are *The Final Rose* kids out there! We can't keep the show running unless it's entertaining.

I leave the trailer. We've decided to choose the girls randomly at the end of the first elimination, throwing Vera's name into the mix as a definite top choice for the date. We all agree it would be better if he ranks Vera high so we have an excuse for putting them together, but we can come up with something else if he doesn't.

I nod and say nothing, shaking myself off and burying my nose in my work where it belongs.

The lights are on Sebastian, and if he hadn't confessed to me he was nervous, I wouldn't know. He looks regal in his blue suit with a pink pocket square. His hair is perfectly brushed back, and his blue eyes shine more than ever.

I bite my nails furiously. I promised I'd let them grow, but here we are.

"Ready, Sosa?" Gary asks, and I nod.

I have an earpiece to hear what they're saying, and my eyes won't leave the scene. Our host, Andrea Fox, is gorgeous, talking to everyone and laughing loudly as she steals glances at Sebastian.

He doesn't notice her. Squaring his shoulders, he checks his sleeves. Only when he's satisfied with the state of his clothes does his gaze wander. To the setting, to the loud host, the cameraman right on his face...to me.

Our eyes lock and I gulp. He smiles and I timidly return it.

I don't know what the hell is wrong with me, but I have to stop. I look away before my cheeks warm or I do something stupid, only to meet a camera pointed in my face.

"What the hell, Will?" I complain.

"You know I like to film pretty things," he tells me with a wink.

I roll my eyes. Will loves filming the crew and usually puts together a little video of us at the end of each season as a job-well-done gift.

"Places," Jeff calls, and everyone straightens up.

My errant eyes find Sebastian. He's looking at me, too.

"Welcome to The Final Rose, the show that will change how you see love," Andrea calls as the cameras roll.

I hold my breath through the first section, but there's no reason to do so. She approaches Sebastian, and they talk easily. He's a bright light on camera, and his accent is even better through the earpiece, like he's murmuring to me. Each syllable is spoken in a purr. The hair on the nape of my neck stands as he drags his vowels.

Of all the beautiful people in Los Angeles, I can't believe this London boy is the one who flusters me.

Andrea goes on and on, as she usually does. When the cameras stop for a retake, she complains about the humidity and Anya yells for someone to turn up the AC—predictable.

In the next section, the girls arrive, and I'm chewing my nails. The first elimination is the one I look forward to the most. It sets the tone for the season and shows us a little bit of how our Eligible thinks. It makes or breaks television.

I used to love this kind of tension, lived for it. But as I watch the episode unfold like its most unwilling participant, I can't recall why the hell I thought this was fun.

"Are you ready, Sebastian?" Andrea asks.

"Yes."

"Sure of your choices?"

"They are all lovely ladies, Andrea. This little time together wasn't enough, but I need to trust..." A beat. "My gut ."

I know it isn't his gut he's trusting. His impossibly blue eyes are zeroed in on me. Cheeks burning, I nearly bite off my entire thumbnail.

The second lasts forever. I want him to trust my judgment.

I'm happy he listened, but at the same time, it dawns on me how much responsibility it actually is.

I know in my bones Sebastian believes in this *The Final Rose* circus. He wants a wife, simple as that. He wants a wife, and now, he trusts me to find him one.

I know the word before it's out of his lips. Andrea looks at the camera and asks Sebastian which girl he wants to see here next week.

My hand drops from my mouth, and I watch and watch and watch.

I should be happy I steered him away from a bad decision.

But I'm not.

Because I'm wondering if I did it for the sake of a good match or ratings. Am I committed to him or the show?

I don't know which is more insane. I want to grab the *The Final Rose* logo embroidered over the breast of my tee and rub it like a talisman. I have to be loyal to the show, not some dude I just met.

The lights are bright. The set is a little cooler now; someone cranked up the AC so the talent doesn't melt. I close my hands in a fist and suddenly pray for him to forge his own way.

I don't want the responsibility anymore. It's not *fun*.

"The first girl I want to see next week is...Vera."

Goddammit.

CHAPTER 6
Sebastian

The girls line up behind me as we all smile at the cameras with annoying sweetness.

For the first time since I threw my hat into the hypothetical ring, I wonder why the hell I even started this.

It might be my mother's voice saying I shouldn't, or maybe my traitorous heart, who's foolish enough to believe in happy endings, but the first elimination leaves a sour taste in my mouth.

I know nothing about them.

Our interactions count for less than a drunken hello in a pub. I've had longer conversations through a bathroom stall than with these women behind me.

Now and again, I glance over at Callie, wanting to find her reassuring smile, but she's chewing on her thumb like there's no tomorrow.

The host says more nonsense to the camera, and after a second, we're done. I'm rooted to the spot, not sure where we can go from here.

Fingers close around my arm, taking me out of my head.

Vera stands there, looking up at me. We let the other girls talk as they shoot small waves and anxious smiles.

They all look stunning today, and Vera fits the part. Her soft caramel hair falls over her shoulder in perfect waves. Her brown eyes hold me captive from the second I face her. She's dressed in a beautiful golden gown that shows exactly who she is. Though garments shouldn't talk, Vera's choices make her glow under the harsh lights.

"I know the normal way to go about this is to thank you for keeping me." Her hand finds the back of her neck like she's struggling to talk.

"You don't need to thank me..."

She steps closer, lowering her voice. "The thing is... I don't know why you did it. We barely talked. I was pretty sure you didn't even know my name. Maybe you thought I was pretty and decided to keep me, and that's fine, but as your first choice?" She takes a second, sucking in a breath before asking, "Is this fixed?"

My lips part with the voracity of her accusation. Her eyes shine, and right then, I know Vera is just like me: a romantic. She's here to fall in love, and being picked first feels wrong if it isn't sincere.

"Sebastian, that blue looks great on you."

The voice has me whipping my eyes from Vera, and once the owner of the voice approaches, the rest of them circle us. The moment is broken. I throw them a media-trained smile to keep things light. Vera watches me in doubt, and my stomach plummets.

In a way, her accusation is true. Callie whispered in my ear to pick Vera, and that's why I did it.

Callie, a producer.

She has access to backstage, to the showrunners. She understands what's happening much more than I do.

As I numbly talk about my choice of suit and how the beverages are indeed heavenly, my mind doesn't rest.

I should take the opportunity to get to meet the girls, but all I can think about is Callie.

Why do I trust her? Why did I let myself forget for a second that she's a producer?

It wasn't long ago when I called Maverick and told him I was going in with my eyes wide open. I would let nothing steer me. No one could put words in my mouth.

Yet, here I am, in the first week, a marionette.

I remove Elliana's bio from the pile and then spread all the pictures across my hotel bed. I take the armchair to the side, my elbows resting on my knees, and I breathe.

Maybe I'm blowing this out of proportion, but I can't shake Vera's insinuation. And what bugs me is that I don't feel manipulated.

Callie told me something, and I followed. No questions asked, no moment where I reminded her this is my life. I should eliminate who I want. I just blindly followed her, and I wonder if it's possible to trust someone so quickly—especially someone you shouldn't. The phone rings, but my eyes never leave the pictures. I don't know why I'm playing the staring game, but I am.

It rings again, and this time, I glance in the direction of the hotel phone. No one knows I'm here but the production, so obviously, it's one of them. I stand up and reach for the bedside table, my pajama bottoms hanging low, my forehead scrunched in a frown.

"Yes?"

"Oh good, you're there."

Her voice fills my ear, and for just a second, I forget I was supposed to be angry. She has a raspy quality to her voice, a little out of breath at times, sassy with a hint of something else.

I close my eyes. "Something wrong?"

"What are you talking about? I promised to call so we can talk about the girls. You said you needed someone."

I said all that, but now, I'm struggling to remember why it was appropriate to confide in a producer. It's the way Callie talks, the way she moves around the set, that almost makes you think she's a friend.

But she's the one conducting the one-on-one interviews, isn't she? It means she's literally paid to make us feel at ease.

I can't forget about that.

"You didn't need to ring me. The elimination is over."

She blows a raspberry. "Well, you have a group date to go on and many more eliminations. So, let's talk."

My chest constricts . My eyes are glued to the pictures of the girls in front of me.

"Sebastian?" her voice calls my name. "Why are you being so weird, dude? What the hell is going on?"

I don't ask how she knows something is wrong with me. Instead, I let out a shuddering breath and give up on the charade.

"Why Vera?"

"Again with this?"

"Why are you pushing so hard for her?"

"I told you, Sebastian. I– "

"That's the thing, Callie. You didn't. You were so against eliminating Vera, but don't you think I deserve to know why?"

"She's lovely and deserves a chance."

"So do any of the girls," I'm quick to reply.

She groans like I'm being impossible. My fingers rake through my hair in irritation.

"Did you ever think this was going to be easy?" she fires back.

"I didn't think–"

"You can't fucking crumble in the first elimination!" I'm taken aback by her ferocity.

"I'm not crumbling!"

I'm the definition of crumbling.

"Oh boy," she scoffs. "You're crumbling like...like..."

"Rhubarb crumble." I'm nothing but helpful.

"Oh, my God, no. Like an apple crumble! Like a cookie! Who the hell thinks about rhubarb first?"

I try to hide my reaction, but her exasperation over the rhubarb makes my lips twitch. Defeated, I sit down on the bed, trying to find a space away from the pictures.

"I didn't think it was going to be this hard," I confess. "I thought I was going to click with people straight away and just follow my instincts. But I was lost there. That elimination had no rhyme or reason. I just said names in no particular order."

She grunts, the phone rustling as she moves around. "I'm going to need wine if I'm going to deal with your idealistic ass."

I chuckle. "Are you home?"

"Yes, in the smallest apartment on the bad side of town."

I remove the photos from my bed. "I thought you had a good job."

"It's an expensive city."

Liquid sloshes as she pours herself a glass, and I ask, "Red or white?"

"Cheap rosé."

"Pink. What a classy lady."

"You can't knock boxed wine until–"

"Boxed wine?!"

"Don't you even start. You a sommelier or something?

Actually, you know what? Don't answer that. I want to keep liking you."

I want to dig deep into this whole liking me business, but she talks again. "Tell me what got your panties in a twist, Riggs."

"Crumbles, panties in a twist. Is it in your job description to emasculate the contestants?"

"No, that's just one of the perks. Out with it. Tell me, or I'll ignore you in favor of any sitcom rerun."

I blow out a breath. Finally, my bed is free of pictures, and I put my feet up, resting my back against the headboard. I know I unraveled because of what Vera said, but I don't want to throw her under the bus.

"Today...it felt rigged."

"Rigged?" She seems to pay attention.

I lift a shoulder she can't see. "You are clearly pulling for Vera, and I don't know your motives. I feel you're steering me one way, and I'm letting you do it because I don't know any better."

I finish talking, and she takes a moment to reply. I know I just poked my finger in the right spot.

"Callie..." I start, but she finally talks again.

"No, no. It's not rigged. But hey, you say you know nothing about them yet? We know plenty. Our casting had loads of interviews with all the girls, and now that I know you, I can match you properly. It's in the show's best interest to see your happy ending."

"So, you truly think Vera is for me?"

"I know she's kind, smart, and adorable in a very real, dorky way."

"And you think that's my type?" I'm messing with her at this point, because she just nailed it. That description is pretty much my type. The girl next door with wit and sarcasm. And maybe shapely legs and a nice bum...

And now I'm imagining Callie and the way her denim shorts fit her perfectly. I'm thinking of her quick comebacks with that throaty voice of hers and the wicked grin she gets when she pulls my leg.

"Listen," she starts, unaware of my unrequited lust. "I get to know a lot of guys, in and out of *The Final Rose–*"

"Let's talk about the ones you met out..."

"Ha! Only your love life may be discussed in these phone calls."

"Who made that rule?"

"Are you drunk? Me! Just now."

I smile. "I didn't know we could make rules willy-nilly like that."

"Riggs, listen to me. I can see you're for real, and she's for real too. I think you both can get along. I'm not saying she's the one. Things change, but I think you should give her a chance."

Her words put me at ease, as much as I don't want to admit it.

It's not Vera or the girl I let go who put me on edge, but how quickly I took Callie's direction. I need to keep my eyes open during this damn show, but instead of protecting myself, I'm here, chatting on the phone with the field producer.

It's just bad all around and makes me feel dumb to take Callie's word . I can't stop myself from accepting her friendship. It's addictive. Every time we banter, I crave more. I can't just keep her at arm's length. I just can't.

"I'm going to give her a chance," I finally agree, like I hadn't promised that before. "We're going on a date, aren't we?"

"With five more people."

I groan. "Callie..."

"Hey, I did my best. It was supposed to be seven girls. You

53

can't have one-on-ones all the time. It's just getting started, and it's a mess at first. There are too many of you, and–"

"And if you can't have a camera on all of our faces, what's the point?"

"It's not as cynical as you believe."

I chuckle. "Do you believe in *The Final Rose?*"

"Sure do. I get a deposit in my bank account every month proving they are indeed real."

"Cute." She laughs at her cleverness. "But if you could be one of the contestants? Or the main single? Would you?"

"I don't think I could be on TV."

"Besides the TV part. I mean, do you think the formula works?"

She sighs before answering, and I imagine her kicking her feet up and thinking about my question.

"It's hard to take the cameras out of consideration because it's a huge part of it. Not just because it's a reality show, you know?" She considers it. "It's because it's part of the formula. Being filmed changes people, makes them consider what kind of person they want to show the world. It amplifies everything like a giant magnifying glass. People do things alone they wouldn't do in front of a camera. I don't mean just the nasty stuff."

"So, it is worse, isn't it? It means people pretend to be good because they're being watched. They aren't real."

"Not necessarily. Yes, we get a few weirdos who are one thing when the lights are on and another when they're off, but when you know you're being watched, you think about your actions more. Even the nicest person would say something hurtful during a fight. But when your first fight as a couple is with cameras in your face? You think through it. And some-times, thinking is all you need to step away and choose less hurtful words. Words you wouldn't regret."

I think of my posed family and see myself nodding. "But it can ricochet. Sometimes, people are media trained and can't ever let it go."

"Well, that clearly isn't you, because I still insist you're too sarcastic to be media trained."

I scoff. "Oh, you stop. I'm English. But yes, I was talking about my family."

She hums on the other side. "Must be nice when your family doesn't say all they think of you in one blow."

"Oh, they say it. It's just in the worst way possible, full of riddles that leave your head hurting trying to figure it out."

"Well, my family is Colombian. Whatever needs to be said, they will say it to your face using small words because they truly believe you're dumb."

I laugh at the way she says it matter-of-factly. She talks again after a chuckle. "I love those dumb-dumbs, but I was just saying, you know, families are weird."

I don't want to go into detail about how my family differs from her lovable *dumb-dumbs*, but I also don't want to finish this phone call. Now would be the best time to thank her for calming me down and let her go.

But I can't.

I want to talk more; I want to hear more about her. I want her to sass me just a little more.

"So, it's a no to *The Final Rose*?"

She laughs. "If I tell you no, would it be me admitting I don't believe in the formula?"

"You can press the number two twice if, by contract, you aren't allowed to say that."

"Dork," she grumbles, and I can almost see her rolling her eyes. "What I'm saying is that reality TV isn't for everyone. I think love can be found anywhere, Riggs. There isn't a map or a foolproof way. Being a fool probably helps a little. It can happen to anyone at any time. You're going down the street one day, and BAM."

"Love hits?"

"Like lightning."

CHAPTER 7
Callie

This flower bouquet is the craziest bunch I've seen so far. With a wide range of color and variety, I'm sure this is the most expensive yet.

I snort a laugh. I can't wait until we pack our bags and go to London for the next stretch of the show so I can meet Maverick. He's either an extremely sentimental friend or the best prankster. Something tells me he's both.

Being as discreet as I can, I glance at my phone and revisit the messages from last night. It's not every night Sebastian calls me, and it's never *preposterously* late, as he claimed at first. But when he doesn't call me, he texts. And it's less and less about the show, which should concern me, but I'm stupid enough to feel charmed.

I've never been stupid enough for anything. I'm a Sosa. We are smart people.

What happened to my intellect remains to be seen, but now, I stride around the mansion with an enormous bunch of flowers resting in the crook of my arm and my hand clasped on my phone.

SEBASTIAN

Why can't I find a decent kebab in this town?

CALLIE

I'm sure you can find a kebab in L.A.

SEBASTIAN

Need a dirty, chippy kebab after getting sozzled.

CALLIE

I don't think those are words.

CALLIE

Aren't you supposed to be royalty, anyway? None of this sounds like something a Prince would say.

SEBASTIAN

Maybe you don't know them well enough. No matter. The Riggs family isn't royalty, but Americans are easily fooled by an accent.

CALLIE

Don't tell casting that.

SEBASTIAN

Riggs are bastards enough to be almost royalty.

CALLIE

I thought being a bastard was a secure way not to get a title.

SEBASTIAN

Semantics.

CALLIE

I just googled sozzled! Sebastian, are you drunk?

SEBASTIAN

...

How can you type, nay, think the word
semantics when you're drunk?

After that, he ended up finding a good enough kebab and
tucked in for the night. I couldn't even blame him for getting
drunk on expensive mini-bar drinks. Being a contestant in a
reality show is boring. While the girls are constantly watched
and called to interact all the time, Sebastian is kept away.

It works for the formula. Let the girls fight over the prize,
who isn't even in the same house, and at the same time, keep
the dates pure and exciting. But the Eligible gets day after day
of doing a bunch of nothing in a hotel room.

Tracing my steps to the back of the mansion, I get in the
middle of the mess going on out there.

Cameras, assistants, and sound mixers swarm the place.
Six girls were chosen for this group date: Vera, Mackenzie,
Vivian, Maya, Abby, and Emily. I tried to get Kirsten
included on the date since she was the production's number
two option, but Anya thought it was good for her to feel
excluded.

I needed to shake myself after that comment.

Something is changing, and it's not my boss or the structure of the show. It's me, and the thought alone is terrifying.

We need drama to keep the lights on. I say it again and
again to myself, but this season, the justification won't stick in
my brain.

The meddling makes my skin crawl. A conscience isn't
something I can have if I'm going to survive in this industry.

The truth is, I can't stop TV from being TV.

But I *can* find someone for Sebastian. I want to do it. I
want to be there for him because he has become a friend. A
weird, sometimes too British one, but a friend, nonetheless.

I march toward him with his ridiculous flower bouquet in

hand. I breathe in the morning air and tell myself I will find this man a wife and clear my conscience in the process.

"Oh, Callie, you shouldn't have, love," he says as I approach.

"I don't even know the names of these flowers, Riggs," I tell him, thrusting the bouquet in his hands. "How can he order so easily from a different continent?"

"Oh, Maverick is resourceful. He'd pride himself on knowing best flower shop in L.A. I'm sure he'll manage to throw it into conversation."

"Name dropping, flower edition." I bite my cheek so as not to smile.

"Precisely."

"We don't do flowers here!" Anya's voice cuts through our conversation from the other side of the backyard.

She doesn't approach, so I have to yell back: "I know!"

"He has flowers. Why does he have flowers?"

"It's a fancy British thing. He insists on smelling the flowers before each date."

I suck on my lips, closing my mouth so I don't laugh when Anya shakes her head. "The fucking English..."

When I turn to Sebastian, he wears the cutest shocked expression, and I have to laugh.

"She believed you!"

"Oh yes, she did."

"I thought your aim was to make me desirable, not a lunatic who absolutely must stop to smell the flowers."

"Smelling the flowers is hardly the craziest request we've had," I say, taking the bouquet from his arms and giving it to an intern—though not before I take the small card on top and hand it to him.

"Still, it doesn't put me in the best light." He reads the card, a little smile curling up his lip.

"Don't worry, you don't have to seduce Anya. You wouldn't survive that."

"Oh, I'm surely not man enough." He passes me the card so I can read too.

"Are you ready for your date?" I ask after finishing with the card.

His eyes trace behind my head to the six girls standing not so far from us. They are all dressed in what can only be described as Golfer Chic, the same as him. It's the first time I've seen him out of a suit, and I'm not sure what to make of it.

The shirt they put on him makes his impossibly blue eyes shine even more. It's almost immoral how absolutely breath-taking this man can be.

"How can one even worry in a situation like this? A date with six women is surely a recurring event in any gentleman's life," he says wryly.

"You put together ridiculous sentences when you're being sarcastic. That's your tell."

"It's the subtitles you wanted for me?"

I nod. "How I can translate that to the audience is anyone's guess."

"I'm sure you'll find a way, being capable and all that."

"Thanks." I deadpan. "That's the nicest thing anyone ever said to me."

"I am a poet in my spare time."

My lips curve in a little smile, but I hold back. "Please, I hope you brought a poem to share with the ladies."

"Do you think it could help my chances of charming someone at...mini golf?"

"Please." I scoff. "Thousands and thousands of men succeeded before you. It's the standard date activity."

"It's unimaginative, you mean."

I blow a raspberry, because he's so very right. Mini golf is the worst date in the history of dates, but it's one easily recreated when there's a little pitch in the back of the mansion. I won't come out and agree with him, so I offer a new angle.

"Going for an activity is the best option for a first date. There will be no awkward silences, no pauses. You can talk about–"

"It's a date with seven people, Callie." His stare punches a blow to my gut. "It's more of a party than a date."

I let myself smile a little. A wire is visible on his lapel, and I'm fixing it before I think better of it. "You'll do fine. And you'll get to know them."

His neck feels warm beneath my fingers, and they linger, feeling the soft material of his shirt. I frown to myself, his warm breath coming out in puffs over my head.

"Tell me then," he murmurs as his voice drops, "what's *your* perfect first date?"

An unwelcome tremor goes up my spine when I glance up at him. We are all about the banter, but sometimes, Sebastian can rotate my world on its axis so quickly, I'm left catching my breath.

Sebastian has a presence about him. His voice can command, and he's doing it right now. His eyes trace my features for a moment too long, and I remove my hands as if they're burning. I step back and crane my head, chin up.

I won't ever answer him.

"I think you're ready to go," I say, clearing my throat. "I'll tell them we can start."

Before he has a chance to respond, I'm turning around and jogging away.

"She's scared of her own voice!"

I hear Vera's voice through a point in my ear. Her laugh is melodic and, when mixed with Sebastian's, it's pure harmony. I never knew laughs could mix and form goddamn music, but I guess I stand corrected.

The date goes well, but my mood sours. Suddenly, everything irritates me—the weather, my co-workers, the contestants, and the blue sky itself.

Abby is the worst golfer of them all. Once she finishes up her shot, Vera turns to her with a good-natured smile. "Is the screeching helping with your game?"

Abby throws her head back and laughs. "Of course, it's helping! I'm your regular Tiger Woods."

I have to admit; the girls are fantastic. They smile, joke, and enjoy themselves. Vera and Abby are definitely the nicest. I can't imagine them turning nasty just for the game's sake.

Vivian and Maya aren't as talkative, preferring to stay on the sidelines and observe. I understand the instinct, but that will hurt them long-term. It's halfway through the date, and we barely have footage of them interacting with Sebastian. Soon, their faces will blend into the background, and folks at home will never remember them.

The only salvation for Vivian and Maya is Mackenzie and Emily. They are...difficult. I try to stay positive and not judge much, but man, they are horrible people.

Emily is a whiner. I'm still waiting to hear her voice without the drag of every final syllable accompanied by a pout.

And Mackenzie is just plain mean. Her comments are hard to ignore. She talks behind everyone's back.

"I can't believe she thinks *that* skirt looks good," she says to Emily, who snickers and slaps her on the arm.

"This girl has a one-way ticket to being the season's villain," Nessa whispers from behind me, a little frown on her forehead, as if it pains her to hear the comments.

"We won't air all that at once. It needs to be built up." I sigh.

The fundamental difference between reality TV and reality is that people in real life reveal themselves the first opportunity they have.

Armed with misguided beliefs, no one sees themselves as the bad guy. Villains don't exist in real life. They are just regular people who think they have the right to suck.

On reality TV, we need to build a little thing called a narrative. It doesn't serve any of us to lay all the cards in the first episode. Even though I know Mackenzie isn't a nice person, I know they will keep her for a long time and unravel her personality, one comment at a time.

I breathe an impatient breath. The words rolling off Mackenzie's tongue are enough to set women back a hundred years. She says awful things about Abby's thighs, is disgusted by Vera's outfit, rolls her eyes every time Vivian talks, and her nasty comments about Maya's hair are downright racist.

If we deliver the actual footage, the internet will eat her alive. I hate that we'll have to sit on this.

I watch the rest of the date when it's the last thing I want to do. Sebastian is back to his royal self: charming, with a velvet accent and a cute little dimple, making the girls fall over themselves for a sliver of his attention.

I bite my cheek as he gives Maya pointers on her pitch. The whole scene is straight out of a romantic comedy, and Nessa squeaks by my side.

"Tell me I'm not a genius for getting Sebastian Riggs?" She elbows me in the gut, and I'm forced to look away from Sebastian to focus on my friend. "England's most eligible bachelor. And look at them! The girls can't believe their luck."

I look away from Nessa again. Maya takes her shot and laughs with Sebastian when it goes as bad as previously.

"He's good," I accept.

"Good?" I hear the scoff in my friend's voice. "He's Prince Charming."

Yes, I get that. He sure looks like Prince Charming and Barbie's Ken all rolled up in one. But he's also sarcastic, witty, and plain annoying when he wants to be. He says incomprehensible words, all laced with unexpected humor.

He's *not* perfect.

He's *not* a character.

He's a three-dimensional being, full of life.

He's actually a pain in my ass.

I'm on my fourth cup of coffee. It's also after 10 pm.

Our crew meeting is full, and since I hate this kind of affair, I concentrate on the whiteboard in front of me, rather than on the rest of the people. Our schedule is laid out from now until the end of the season, every episode accounted for, every twist and turn planned.

I used to love the feeling of reality TV twisting the old, plain reality. I liked the thrill of planning what couldn't be planned, the race when things turned bad without warning.

I'm disconnected from this season, though, and I feel it all over my skin. The weird feeling churning in my belly is one I can't understand.

I love my job. I'm good at it. I like the crew, and I believe in the show. I count all the ways why I should be comfortable, but still, something turns me inside out.

I'm forced to stop addressing my nerves. I'm in a room full of people, and things turn up a notch when Adam arrives and goes straight to the board. With no ceremony, he wipes all our schedules dramatically. I don't gasp; it's not like we don't have it penciled in our journals, laptops, emails, and everywhere else.

He grabs the black marker and writes right in the middle of the whiteboard:

Vera

Kirsten

Maya

Mackenzie

He drops the marker as he swirls around to face us.

"Who else?"

Someone from Nessa's team clears her throat. "I'd say Abby instead of Kirsten. She's lively and did well on the group date."

"We need six names to bring to London. Why not just add her?"

"Abby and Kirsten are equivalents." Someone waves me off.

I frown, but I say nothing. In real life, no two people are interchangeable. But on TV?

Abby and Kirsten are sweet brunettes who work with children. If this was a fiction series, their stories would be mashed into one character.

"Let's wait for the screen test," Anya speaks up. "And go with the one who tests better."

Adam agrees, and besides Kirsten's name, he adds a "slash Abby."

"How about the southern belle?" Devi asks.

"Oh!" Nessa taps her pen happily on the table. "She has never left the country!"

"That's a great segment." And Grace is added to the list.

"One more name, people."

If I was dumber, I'd point out that Sebastian is the one choosing who he's bringing to London.

We traditionally take the top six and the Eligible on a romantic trip to the Canary Islands for the second leg of the show, but since Sebastian is from London, the opportunity was too good to pass up.

Instead, we'll have him in his environment with hopefully plenty of footage of the girls trying to fit into his life.

"Emily is annoying," Olivia, the other camera assistant, points out. "I bet she can complain about London until the cows come home."

Adam tsks. "We are keeping Mackenzie, but we need to give the public some satisfaction of a good elimination. They both behaved poorly on the group date, but Sebastian heard Emily's whining while he didn't know Mackenzie was talking about everyone behind their backs."

"We can't keep all the bad people," Anya agrees. "It's great for a storyline, but we all know the public gets frustrated when bad behavior goes unpunished. We need to give them closure, and Emily will be the sacrificial lamb."

I sigh and bring my elbows resting on the table.

"What do you think, Sosa?" Anya watches me in the most intense way. "You spend time with him the most."

She's not exactly calling on me, but I feel a chill down my spine nevertheless. My job is to be close to the contestants, but I bet what's bugging her is that I'm not reporting as much as I used to.

It's not that I'm loyal to Sebastian over Anya.

No.

I just have nothing to add to the conversation. That's what I tell myself, anyway. When I clear my throat to talk, my mouth is cotton dry, and my leg twitches under the table.

"Who's left?" I stall.

"Isla, Vivian, and Summer," Nessa replies promptly.

"I'd say Vivian then," I tell them, not really thinking about it.

Adam crosses his arms over his chest. "Why?"

"She did ok during the group date. She's nice, but it's not like she will make it to the finale. You need fat to trim."

"I think that's a bad idea," Olivia opposes. "It will look like it was set from the first elimination."

"How?" I ask, resting my back on the chair.

"In the first elimination, we got names for the group date. We have footage of Isla and Kirsten talking about how they think Sebastian chose. We need to shake them off the scent. Vivian and Maya were on the group date, but they weren't particularly remarkable. It's Vivian *or* Maya."

I blow a raspberry. "Well, no offense, but we have a white-ass cast as it is. You can't eliminate the only Black girl." I'm still salty that not one single Latina was chosen for this season.

"So, Maya stays." Adam nods, tapping his finger over her name already written on the board.

"It's Isla or Summer." Anya pins us with a look that ends on me. "A coin toss."

I think back on my interactions with Sebastian, but he said nothing about either of them. It's still too early in the game.

"Can we wait for him to decide?" I finally say. "We have it narrowed down to two anyway."

Anya watches me for a second too long, but she nods. "Sosa is right. We nudge those connections on the board but leave Summer and Isla be. Look at us, leaving it all to fate and shit." She laughs ,and the rest of the crew follows suit.

Adam seems to be satisfied, and we are allowed to finally leave. My back is sore where the bra straps dig into my skin, my face feels oily and disgusting, and all I can think about is a shower and at least four hours of uninterrupted sleep.

I'm going down the stairs as quickly as I can when Anya

calls my name. I squeeze my eyes shut, but I wait for her at the bottom.

I did nothing wrong; I know that. I'm feeling weird, sure, but that's not a reason to fire someone. I'm probably too tired and too emotional for whatever reason. Soon, I'll be back in the game.

Anya nods toward the back door, glancing around so we aren't overheard. While this side of the mansion works for us as an office, we can't forget the rest is where the girls live and are being filmed.

We slip to the backyard, but Anya doesn't stop. We walk further away from the porch, past the jacuzzi toward the mini golf pitch. When we finally stop, she crosses her arms over her chest, and I almost feel naked at the look she gives me.

"Never saw you so quiet during a meeting."

I shrug. "This time around seems to be more set."

Anya tsks. "Funny, because I think exactly the opposite. Other Eligibles come here with an ulterior motive. They have no problem judging the girls by their looks, but Riggs? He's a wild card."

"He's an English aristocrat. There's nothing wild about him." I snicker.

"He doesn't play by the rules, and you know it." I turn my face away, refusing to reply, so she keeps going. "Now more than ever, we need to tug on the reins and steer to the right side. *Dating Blind* is breathing over our necks."

I turn to her again. *Dating Blind* is the other popular dating reality show, but there, the contestants know nothing about each other before meeting. Our tagline is that *The Final Rose* is *the show that changes how you see love*. Well, that's no longer true.

"You know we are just one bad season away from cancellation," Anya actually admits. "Every show is always half a season from cancellation. Nowadays, people want immediate results. If it doesn't go viral, if it doesn't shock or turn hella messy, people don't care about it."

"I thought that's why it was so good to get someone like Sebastian." I finally find my voice.

"Prince Charming is a good start, but you know one person doesn't make a season."

I move uncomfortably. "I know, Anya. I don't understand why we're having this conversation."

"We are having this conversation because your head is not in the game. Each season, you become laser-focused. You know them inside out; you nudge them in the direction you want. You craft those lines better than the writing staff."

I feel my cheeks burn, and I thank God it's dark so she doesn't see it. I used to preen under Anya's compliments. They were few and far between, but now, all I want is for her to stop talking.

"I want you glued to Vera and Kirsten. I want you to make those girls the princesses for that Prince Charming."

The order is so direct, I don't know how I'm able to croak out another sentence. But once I do, I know it's a mistake.

"If it's not them? If he likes Summer, Vivian, hell, even Mackenzie?"

Her eyes narrow. "Then you make him see the light."

She turns around, but I stay. With a last look over her shoulder, she says, "You better be back to normal by the time you're on that plane to London."

CHAPTER 8
Callie

"It makes no sense anyway. It's not like Mackenzie knows what really happened."

I rub my temple, nodding my head. Before I have a chance to say anything, Summer continues. "There's nothing to it. People wouldn't bring us here just to be judged that way. It's about what Sebastian wants, and he gave no–"

"Can you just calmly tell me what happened?" I ask, pointing to the camera.

I've been with Summer for a solo interview for the last twenty minutes, but she's talking a mile a minute, and we can't use any of it if she doesn't start making sense ASAP.

I take a deep breath in, signaling she should follow my lead. With her mouth clamped shut like it's an effort, she does. I smile and then roll my finger forward, telling her she can start.

Hopefully, this time, she will start from the beginning.

"Well, last night after we came back from the pool hang, Mackenzie was doing her makeup and talking loudly with Emily about some of her theories. She was saying the girls who weren't invited to the first group date were included in the pool hang so Sebastian could decide who he was eliminating next."

I wish she would stop calling it "the pool hang", but Mackenzie isn't completely wrong. She missed the part that every date can seal the deal. It wasn't exclusively the pool hang. Damn, now she has me calling it that too.

After the mini-golf date, Sebastian still wanted to get to know the other girls. It's hard for him, apparently, as he can't stop complaining, but not every date in *The Final Rose* will be super cute. There are thirsty women out there, and we have to make a show for them too.

So, we took Sebastian's shirt off and sent him to the pool with a few girls, including Summer. Once everyone returned to their rooms, instead of asking how it went, Mackenzie staged a conversation with Emily where she shared theories about the elimination process.

That's how I ended up here this late at night. I have to get the interviews before everyone has a chance to sleep on it and realize Mackenzie is simply talking out of her ass.

"If I was going to believe her, I'd have to accept that he's had a favorite since day one! That's not how it works!"

Since Summer's speculations of how the show works don't exactly make for good TV, I steer her away from it. "Why do you think Mackenzie said what she said?"

"Jealousy." Summer replies promptly. When I point in the camera's direction, she licks her lips and tries again. "I think Mackenzie is jealous."

"Mackenzie is trying to scare us," Isla says in her solo interview, half an hour after I'm finished with Summer. "She wants to see everyone on their toes. The glory of being selected for the first group date didn't last long enough."

"The other girls think she's jealous. Were you jealous when you weren't invited to the first group date?" I ask.

Isla shrugs. "We all want an opportunity to get to know Sebastian, but I really don't think fighting is the solution."

She clearly doesn't understand how reality TV works. I nod anyway because, at this point, I'm beyond tired. At least I got the nice girls' interview. Anya is dealing with Mackenzie and Emily right now, and while I wish I was a bug in that room, I'm happy to be spared.

"You look tired," Vera tells me while she's being mic-ed.

I huff a laugh. "Thanks. You look gorgeous."

"I mean, the dark shadows under your eyes completely work for you. You go, girl," she jokes, and I laugh for the first time since this mess started.

Not that I don't love a good drama, but Mackenzie could've waited until the morning to spread lies. I've been in the mansion since dawn; the twenty-four-hour mark is approaching. I'm tired and in need of a shower, but I also get that sometimes, things like this happen. Sometimes, we can't leave interviews for the next day.

Once Vera is ready to go, I start. "Tell me what was happening in the room when the girls were at the pool hang."

Vera wrinkles her nose. "Are we calling it that?"

I blow a raspberry and raise a hand. I gave up fighting it.

Shaking her head, Vera starts. "From the moment the group date was announced, Mackenzie thought she was going to be included. She was showing her two-piece to Emily and said she couldn't wait to hang with Sebastian by the pool. When they sent the names, I thought it was obvious. We had our date already, and now it was an opportunity for the other girls to connect with Sebastian, but Mackenzie was really annoyed by that. She made—"

She stops herself mid-sentence, and I frown. I like interviews with Vera because she's always the voice of reason. She tells us how it is, making my job much easier, especially when I need to perform through the night.

"What's wrong?" I ask.

"She made a few comments about Grace's body and why she shouldn't be in a bikini."

I close my mouth in a firm line. I'm not going to say that *The Final Rose* is inclusive, because it's not. The show has a long way to go until it shows regular bodies on TV, but it has improved immensely since the first season. Grace is cute as a button, short, blonde, and perky. She's our southern belle who likes horseback riding and has the nicest accent. She has the body to do the activities she's interested in.

Good for her. *I hate Mackenzie.*

I hate that every season, we need to have a villain, and she's fitting too well into the role. I hate that she talks like that about the other women, even if it's good television. I'm done with people like that.

Vera frowns, releasing a long breath. "I don't want to talk about that. I don't want to expose Grace like that. She heard what Mackenzie said. She can say something if she wants."

I nod, getting what she's asking. Vera is always happy to retell everything that happens with scientific precision, but we need to be careful with comments about someone's body. Vera doesn't want to victimize Grace, and I get it. Against my *The Final Rose* training, I nod, promising I won't push the subject.

Once we're done, she hugs and thanks me, but I'm not too sure what I'm being thanked for.

And then, I interview Grace, who simply skims through Mackenzie's comments, showing she's not interested in giving the woman extra screen time. Mostly, Grace is upset that Mackenzie and Emily are trying to spoil everyone's fun. Grace is easy-going like that.

I leave the interview room when the sun is peeking over the horizon. *I can't believe I finished all the interviews*, I think as I close my eyes and sag against the wall. I managed to be supportive, connect with the girls, and stay away from Sebastian.

I groan as thoughts of him enter my mind.

After Anya talked to me, I promised to show her my commitment. I came back the next morning with laser focus. A machine called Callie Sosa.

Mackenzie's big mouth was great for my plans. It kept me occupied, my focus on the girls and the girls only.

Head in the game, Callie!

I watch the morning crew arrive and the night cameramen go. I stay in my little trance, deciding if I should push for another couple of hours on set until I crash or just throw in the towel now.

My thoughts are interrupted when the front door swings open, and Sebastian waltzes in with a big cup of coffee in hand.

It's like lightning moving through my body. I jump outside my skin. My hand finds a door handle, and I yank it open without looking where I'm going.

When I close the door, darkness takes over, and I realize I just locked myself in a closet.

I breathe through my nose, my hand over my chest, trying to control my heart rate.

I can't do this. *God, and if I can't do this?*

This is my job. Sebastian is my job. I don't have time to hide from him.

On the other hand, staying with the girls is my job, too. Eventually, living together and competing gets under everybody's skin. I'll be busy as fights and disagreements sparkle through the mansion. For the next few weeks, I'll be a single mother to my overly grown and very misbehaving children.

Biting my lip, I stay put while I hear Sebastian go about his day, saying good morning to the crew and preparing for today's schedule.

Anya knows something weird is going on, and if I'm being honest with myself, I know it too. Something strong pulls me to Sebastian. It takes one second, and he's able to disarm me.

I can't let this take over my life.

Avoiding Sebastian isn't going to be a big deal. I'll concentrate my efforts on the girls. Other people can keep an eye on him.

The closet door swings open, and of course, Sebastian is there. I gulp, and he watches me with humor I don't appreciate. His mouth curves gently as he holds the door open.

"Someone saw you getting in here, but they thought, why would Callie stay that long in a closet?"

I swallow a lump. "I'm checking on something."

"Care to share what?"

"No."

"No? So it's a secret?"

"It's not a secret. You're just not invited to know."

"Damn, you're cranky in the morning."

I sigh, pinching the bridge of my nose. "I'm always cranky."

"Do you want me to bring you coffee?"

"No, just close the door."

He stops for a second. "This door?"

"Can you close the door, please?" I ask again, my eyebrows raised.

"And leave you in a closet in the dark?" I bite my cheeks, refusing to join in on this joke. He looks at me like I'm no fun, his eyes shining.

"Yes, I'd love if you—"

"No problem," he says and swings the door closed.

As soon as it clicks close, I groan. This is stupid. If I'm this bad at avoiding him, I won't last a minute. Now, I'm in the dark, in a goddamn closet, for no good reason. If I'm going to put real distance between Sebastian and me, it needs to be because I know deep in my bones that we must establish some boundaries.

I take a second preparing to see the world. I don't owe anyone an explanation. I can just go back in there and–

The door swings open again. I'm ready to cuss Sebastian, but it isn't him looking back at me. It's Anya.

She frowns, a denim jacket in her hands. We look at each other for a second longer than comfortable, and then she hands me the jacket, assuming I'll hang it up for her.

"I don't like how weird you're getting."

And then, she closes the door in my face.

Awesome, Callie. Awesome.

I drive to my parents' home because it's Saturday, and the weekend is a great excuse to eat Mom's food, and I don't want to be alone right now. I'm full of nervous energy from being awake too long.

I had an energy drink while I waited for the morning traffic to clear, and then I got into the car. I shouldn't have. I was hiding in a closet not too long ago; that's a clear sign of insanity. My mom can sniff that shit out a mile away.

My cheeks burn with shame when I think about how ridiculous it went with Sebastian today. If I want to keep my job, I need to find a way to relax and take a step back.

I hate the feeling of being watched, and that's how I've felt since Anya called me out. Like she saw something I wasn't ready to admit to myself.

I'm different this season because he's here. I'm not ready to face that.

Thankfully, I arrive at my parents' home. As soon as I park

and open the door, I hear music coming from my old neighborhood.

This place is the complete opposite of *The Final Rose* mansion. It feels hotter here, sunnier, homier. On the weekends, everyone is working on their lawns, people coming and going from their weekend jobs, and a couple of barely legal ones are obsessively cleaning their cars with loud music on.

"Ah, Callie! Looking good."

I turn to the right as Raul wiggles his eyebrow and bites his lips, crossing his arms over his chest in front of the most ridiculous altered car I've ever seen.

"I was your babysitter, Raul!" I roar as I open the house's small gate.

"And I remember every minute!" He doesn't give up, even when I laugh and open Mom's front door.

Inside, things aren't that different. Mom is playing music in the kitchen as she makes *tamales* like she does every weekend.

Coming here was a good idea after all.

Mom is singing and dancing away as I put my arm around her midsection, holding her close. Her hands grip me. "Oh, hello, Calliope."

"How do you always know it's me?" I release her, but not before giving her a kiss on the cheek.

"Because my Callie smells like flowers." She smiles, turning around to see me. "And because the other options are three men, I can tell the difference."

I chuckle, and she takes my chin between her fingers. I'm not quick enough to escape, and she's turning my head toward the light, watching me with narrowed eyes.

"You look tired."

"I'd like people to stop saying that." I step away from her hands.

"Who else is saying you look tired?"

"No one, Mom." I groan. "Can I help with the cooking?"

She grunts, turning to the counter again. "You need a nap, no? How late did you work yesterday?"

Mom hates that none of us have nine-to-five jobs. She's proud of hard work, whatever it is, but she worries. She thinks Saturdays are for the family and Sundays are for church. Even though Dad had always worked weekends, she still lectured us anyway.

"I work hard. Aren't you proud?" I deflect by bumping my hip with hers, swaying with the music.

"I'm proud of all my children." She nods. "I'd be prouder if they knew when to quit."

"Sosas aren't quitters, Mami," I joke.

She arches her eyebrows and scoffs. "Come on then. You can't tell me you're too tired to help now, or I get to lecture you about working too hard."

"Of course, I can help," I lie through my teeth.

I don't last long. When I open my mouth on a third yawn, she sends me to the sofa for a nap. I don't get a lecture, only a kiss on my temple as she says, "You can't make good decisions if you're tired."

And she must be right, because when I close my eyes, I only see Sebastian and how little I want to step away from him.

CHAPTER 9
Sebastian

No one knows I changed my ticket to economy. I guess I never bothered to let them know.

The rest of the cast will go first class, but for everyone's sake, I need time away from Mackenzie. Our intimate date two days ago only cemented that I do not know why she's here.

She has been sending me lascivious looks since I got to the airport, so I'm going to guess it went brilliantly from her point of view.

I don't know why I'm bringing Mackenzie. I don't know why, of all the girls, she's 1/6 of my pick. It's like one day, I woke up with no control over my life.

I have always been very certain of my choices. Coming to *The Final Rose* was a risk, but a calculated one. It doesn't feel like that anymore.

I go on dates I don't want to go. I spend time with people I don't really care about. Sure, I enjoy Vera and Abby's company, but I don't crave it. I feel like I should crave it.

But the worst part of this mess is *her*.

Three weeks ago, I found the only person I could trust on

this side of the world. Unapologetically real, Callie Sosa is a beam of light.

Now, she hurries after the rest of the crew like she can't possibly pass through airport security beside me. That is just an example of how the last couple of weeks have been.

I don't know what happened to her, but she changed. One day, like a light switch, *everything* changed.

She avoids me at all costs, and when she has no other option but to deal with my presence, all we talk about is the girls. She avoids any banter and ignores every attempt to be real.

She doesn't deliver Maverick's flowers anymore. Instead, it's the same mousy intern who can't look me in the eye. And even once when I tried to show her what he sent, she got flustered and escaped.

She's distanced herself from my interviews too. Now, I have Anya, who, even though she's short and rude, is excellent at doing her job. She's crafty at getting statements out of me in a way I'm not so comfortable about.

Callie is all about the girls. In their interviews, she's present. I see them exchanging rushed words all over the mansion.

No words are addressed to me.

It's pissing me right off.

I hate the hotel and its white walls. I hate the food and I'm tired of the constant hot weather. I'm ready to go back home.

Maverick is ecstatic. He can't wait to see the set and is hinting at an interview. At least one of us is excited about this whole thing, which proves how things have changed.

Once I'm out of security, I rush trying to get a glimpse of Callie's brown hair, but she's small, the airport is full, and she's hiding from me.

I hear people by my side, but it's only when Abby trips and

I hold her just in time that I realize the girls are around me. I help her up and offer to grab her bag, which she accepts. Grace calls me a true gentleman, and I offer her a closed-lip smile.

Grace is another one who is lovely and polite, but sometimes, I wonder why she's here. We don't click. At all. Everything she says to me is superficial. Not because she's shallow. No, she's lovely, but we have nothing to say to each other.

I shake myself, feeling all too cynical.

My other eliminations weren't as hard as the first, primarily because I got to know them better and realized it isn't because someone's nice that I have to feel attracted to them.

Eliminating them based on our interactions made me feel better, but now that only half of the girls remain, the feeling truly soured.

None of them are my wife.

I came to that acceptance after Summer's elimination. I'm not sure what exactly triggered it, but suddenly, I was painfully aware I should be more interested.

I should feel something. Desire, passion, interest. But I was coming up with nothing.

It became easy to eliminate, because now, it's a game for me too. I don't feel like I'm making a mistake anymore. I know with all certainty that I'm not eliminating my wife.

The weeks after my realization dragged by. Callie continued to ignore me, and I kept polite conversation with the girls I was supposed to be falling in love with.

The group dates I thought I was going to hate, I learned to love. At least during them, the girls chat amongst themselves, even to the point where I feel like an outsider.

They flank me now, asking questions about London and my country house, where a good part of the episodes will be shot.

I laugh at their questions and wish I could stop feeling like this.

Like *The Final Rose* is a mistake.

It's only when we board the plane that I breathe easily. I don't even think about it. I just go straight to my new seat right there in the back with the rest of the mortals. I bring my hand luggage down the aisle, and when I arrive at row twenty-four, I stop and smile at Callie by the window.

She looks up, widening her eyes. "What's wrong?"

I shrug, relaxed, opening the compartment and putting my luggage with hers. "Nothing's wrong."

Callie looks from one side to the other. "You can't sit here."

"Why not? This is my seat."

She is still looking around like the plane police are coming to arrest us at any moment.

"You're supposed to be with the rest of the cast in the first class."

"Funny. That's not what my ticket says." I chuckle as she snags the ticket from my hands, sucking in a breath when it's clear I'm not lying.

"What the hell did you do?" she whisper-shouts.

"Nothing. Are you a chatty Cathy during flights?" I ask, sitting beside her.

"Am I—" She shakes her head. "You need to go back to first class."

"I can't. I don't have a first-class ticket. They wouldn't let me sit there."

"Sebastian, do you understand..." And that's when I see she's truly distressed. I feel like a prick, and I turn my body toward her.

"I just wanted a little company during the flight, ok? It's a long one."

She blows a raspberry. It's her signature move, like she's

physically trying to get rid all the tension on her shoulders as she blows the air out. Her shoulders fall, and she nods, bringing her fingers to her temple.

"It's ok. I just thought you wanted time with the girls away from the cameras."

I guess she's right. I have ten hours without a camera in my face, but instead of using it to get to know the women I'm dating, I switched my ticket and charmed the check-in girl to put me right beside Callie Sosa.

I shrug off the implication. I know well why I don't want to spend more time with them, but I don't tell Callie.

"I just need time away from being that."

"That?"

"The Eligible."

"Oh."

When I look at her, she's nibbling her lips. It's cute. Callie usually looks capable and in control. It's not often I catch her looking vulnerable.

"Did you bring any games?" I ask at the same time as she says, "Do you want to talk about the date?"

I make a disgruntled sound. "My date with Mackenzie?" She nods. "Have you watched it?"

That's another thing. Callie is never around during my dates. She vanishes into thin air. Funny for someone who only wants to talk about them.

She nods, confirming something I already knew. She watches all the dates. Taking notes or whatever, I bet. *Perv.*

"She's..." I don't have words to explain what Mackenzie is. Eventually, I find them. "She's like many women I've met before." Callie's eyebrows rise, and I elaborate. "She worries about looking posh."

"That's what she said to you? I'm Mackenzie and I worry about being posh?"

She laughs like it's the most ridiculous thing she ever

heard. Mackenzie might not have used those exact words, but she wasn't far from it.

I let my head fall to the headrest and close my eyes. When I open them, Callie is watching me.

"I can tell she has all these rules of how to behave," I elaborate. "She follows them and expects everyone else to do so. All she talked about was unimportant things, how to be perceived."

Callie nods. "Yeah, I mean, I don't know how you kept a straight face during that date." She winces. "I stopped watching after the first ten minutes."

"I hope she's not edited too roughly."

I can see by the grimace on Callie's face that that's exactly what's going to happen. "No one put words in her mouth. She said them. In a very dull, horrible monologue. But to be fair, you look like someone who'd like talking about those things."

"About the best restaurants to go to? And the proper places to be seen?"

"She did not list the proper places to be seen!"

I shake my head. "No, but when she told me about a restaurant she liked, she added we can only order in because we can't possibly be seen on that side of town."

"Oh, I bet it's just beside my apartment," she jokes.

"I'd imagine you live just above a Chinese restaurant? Like in the movies?"

She sighs with a dreamy look. "But the owners are simple, hardworking people who like me very much and always give me a doggie bag."

"And even if you went to the posh part of town, you'd miss your true friends, " I finish with my hand resting on my chest.

She actually snorts and doesn't apologize for it. "I'm sure that's a rom-com movie."

I agree. "Yeah, she's going to fall in love with the billionaire and show him money isn't everything."

Callie groans and rolls her eyes dramatically. "That's rich people talking. I'm telling you; money isn't everything, but it would surely fix most of my problems."

"You should ask for a raise. You work too much," I tell her. I don't even know how much she makes, but for what she works, I know it isn't enough.

"We all work a lot. It's television." She pins me with a look. "I could afford a better place, but I'm saving."

"Oh, tell me, Miss Sosa. What are your hopes and dreams?" I perch up my elbow over the armrest and tilt my head on top.

"You know, people look at you, handsome, rich, and with a great accent, and wonder how the hell this man is still single? Well, Riggs, that's why."

I sober up, looking right into her big brown eyes. "No one gets to know me enough to see this part, Callie. They never let me be me enough to get to the–"

"Dorky parts," she interrupts.

I scoff and shake my head. "But you. You're the only one."

The second the words are out of my mouth, I know I made a mistake. Callie blinks a thousand times in a second, her whole body going rigid. It's like a malfunctioning robot. I'd make fun of that if I wasn't so scared to fuck up again.

I don't know why Callie changed with me, and I know if I ask, she'll play crazy. She built a wall over the last weeks, and I can't figure out why. But I don't want her to do it again.

Callie is something I never thought was possible. I'm at ease in her presence. I'm me. And I'll respect any boundaries if it means enjoying her company again.

Trying to bring her back, I clear my throat and ask again, "What are you saving for?"

"What?" She blinks some more.

"What are you saving for?" I repeat.

"Oh." She has a lump in her throat. "I want to buy a house for my parents. They still rent, and I know Dad says they are ok, but..."

"You want to give them something."

She nods, licking her lips. "I'm first generation. Mom and Dad worked their whole lives to give us everything they could, and now that we're grown...it's the least we can do."

"We?" I ask. "Do you have siblings?"

She bobs her head. "Two idiot brothers. They have a construction company together. Our old neighborhood isn't the safest place, but my parents have been living there for the last thirty years and they won't move." She flicks her wrist, showing me it's an ongoing argument with the Sosas. "But we found something affordable and big enough. Comfortable. Ben and Dario say they can work on it if we buy. It's old, but..."

She stops herself from talking, and a small smile tugs at her lips.

"Ben, Dario, and Callie," I test their names.

"Benicio, Calliope and Dario," she corrects me.

"Ah, you're the middle child, Calliope?"

"You're not allowed to call me that."

I smile. "Why?"

"Because that's Dad's privilege."

I shrug. "It's your name."

After a second, she talks again. "Does anyone call you Seb?"

"Mother never liked nicknames very much."

"Oh, she would hate a Latino household. I barely remember most of my cousins' real names, just whatever insane word their friends call them up and down the street.

I can't stop smiling. It sounds like she has a normal life. Friends, a loving and crazy family. It's almost ridiculous how deliciously normal it all sounds. Every child should grow up like that. A bunch of cousins, nicknames, friends, and family. I bet her mother cooks well and her father dotes on her, that her brothers are overprotective and she drinks boxed wine with her friends.

"I thought old British ladies called themselves Birdie and Bunny..." She wriggles her nose in an attempt at an English accent, and I chuckle.

"One has to be creative when every other person is called Margaret or Elizabeth."

"Is Sebastian an original or..." She doesn't even get to finish, and I'm shaking my head.

"My grandfather was Sebastian, as my father is George, like his grandfather. I'm assuming I need to have an heir called George to keep the lineage strong."

"It's the oldest English witchcraft, after all." Callie bobs her head.

We are both chuckling when the plane takes off. I see her clutching the armrest, but I don't say anything, I just watch her expression in silence. Eventually, we stabilize, and they turn off the lights, forcing us to sleep and magically wake up on a different continent. Callie lowers her voice, her head turned to me.

"They hate that you're here."

They are my parents. It's not a question, either. It isn't very hard to see that my parents, being who they are, hate the fact that I'm part of a reality TV show.

"The thing about people like my parents is that they map the lives of their offspring before we are even born. At first, you push yourself to be the best, to keep in line, to make *their* dreams come true. But soon, you're not a child anymore, and their expectations never waver. It's the college they want, the company. The clothes, the events. The job."

Callie frowns and sighs, apparently exhausted on my behalf. *"Contenta, alimentada, y honesta."*

I blink at her. "What's that?"

"The only three things my parents ever wished for me."

Happy, fed, and honest. For the first time in weeks, I want to be in Los Angeles. I want to ask to meet her parents. I want to see her brothers and try to make them like me. I want to help buy her parents a home.

Desperate under my collar, I realize I'm going the wrong way.

It's bluntly cruel how London is the memory of my failures. All the times I wasn't even close to what is expected of a Riggs. All the times I tried and failed. Good TV or not, bringing prospects to London is a mistake, because London's Sebastian Riggs isn't someone I want to be anymore.

He isn't someone who would be the Eligible for *The Final Rose.*

Production wanted to know a little bit about my life. Since my parents refused to be part of it, I arranged for a stay at my country house, take the girls around London and get Maverick to join us and give him the screen time he so badly wants.

But as I imagine myself going back to that house, riding one of my horses and showing them around, I keep thinking about what Callie will think. Is she going to see the beauty of the house for itself or only as a representation of my family's wealth?

Will she be comfortable? Will she think less of me when I show her London's Sebastian?

She wriggles her hands on her lap, uncomfortable by my prolonged silence.

"Do you have siblings?" she asks when it's clear I'm not saying anything else.

I nod dumbly. "Beatrice."

"Younger or older?"

"Younger." I smile. "I want to meet with her while we're there. Off-camera. She's at uni, technically an adult, but I don't want my mother finding reasons to be cross at her. Right now, I'm enemy number one."

Callie blinks with a furrowed forehead. She breathes out and nods. "Yeah, sure. I get it."

"You'll still get to meet her," I guarantee.

"Me?"

I scoff. "Of course. I'll ring her, and we can go for a pint."

Her throat works. "No cameras?"

"No cameras."

And for some reason, I hold my breath. My eyes lock on hers, and I don't dare move.

Finally, Callie nods.

"That'll be great."

CHAPTER 10
Callie

I tug the beanie past my brows. My hands shake when a gust of cold wind cuts through. I'm told this is the mild season, but my Californian ass is freezing, and I'm pretty sure by the glint in Sebastian's eyes, he's relishing in my misery.

I usually like filming outside, but this is different. I hate the cold and wet wind on my face, but I love where we are.

Sebastian was tasked with creating perfect dates to take each girl on, to show them around London. And of course, like everything he does, he nails it.

I bite my lip, trying to keep the pure envy out of my face. I'm walking alongside Justin, the boom man, my earpiece secure in my ear as we follow the adorable couple.

Vera and Sebastian.

She looks glorious in a mid-length, emerald green skirt and a black jacket that is the elevated version of my own. She laughs, throwing her soft caramel hair back, an arm looped around Sebastian's as they talk and walk down the lane.

This little alley, moments from Leicester Square, is a treasure. And sure, at first I made a face when he told us to bring poor Vera for a date in an alley, and I had to remind him we weren't that kind of show. But this date? It's nothing short of perfection.

The alley is a secret spot for second-hand bookshops that, in fifty years, haven't changed their fronts. It's like stepping back in time, every single shop front taking my breath away.

Sebastian handed Vera a cup of coffee and now is letting her browse all she wants. Her fingers trail each spine while she comments on each title.

It's not that I want to be on this date. Of course not.

It's just that this place is a hidden gem, and instead of smelling the books myself, I'm here listening to other people gush about it.

Sebastian is also annoying me.

His accent grew thicker once we landed, and his mannerisms are perfectly timed. He says the right things, smiles on the right cues, and asks insightful questions.

With her, he's not a sarcastic pain in the ass.

He's supposed to show her his real self, right? They are supposed to fall in love, but how can Vera fall in love if he keeps her at arm's length?

That's why I'm so annoyed. Because clearly, I'm more committed to this whole thing of finding him a wife than he is.

Hiding who he is means not giving Vera a fair chance. And if he's not going to give Miss Perfect a chance, what the hell is he even doing?

And God, she's *perfect*. Like right now, as she walks like the most beautiful dream, talking about her super important and difficult STEM job. Even *I* want to marry her.

"Sosa, get going."

I'm ushered inside a bookshop when Jeff announces we have enough footage from the outside. Honestly, this whole thing is a bookworm's wet dream, and I'm getting more envious with each step.

I can't even remember the last time I read a book. Like an actual book, not a script or a magazine. It was probably the *Pretty Little Liars* books in middle school.

But liking books is a state of mind. I do wish I could read more. I do wish I could stop to smell the pages.

I don't know why my lack of reading time is suddenly Sebastian's fault, but it is. So are my cracking lips and chipped nails. I'm trapped in my bad mood, and now, even the way I look bugs me.

I pass a storefront and fix my outfit. And then, I need to shake myself off.

This is not me.

I don't care about any of that. If I did, I wouldn't be working on a show where everyone is literally beautiful enough to burn your retinas.

I'm a Sosa. I'm all about hard work, junk food, and late-night TV. My nail polish is *always* chipped because, as much as I love to see them in color, I don't have time to keep them up.

My hair plays in a weird mix of wavy and curly, depending on the day's humidity. My legs are strong because they bring me up and down the set, and everything about my body is about sustaining my brain.

That's me. But as I walk to Sebastian and Vera, I feel like crap.

A small and ugly pimple on the beautiful canvas of London.

As I approach, Sebastian seems to be the funniest guy in the world, since Vera laughs big, her hands clutching his arm for dear life.

I halt at the sound of her laugh. Maybe interrupting them is a bad idea, but it's too late when Sebastian sees me. His mouth opens in an obscene smile, and his eyes twinkle. I bite the side of my cheek and promise I won't be petty enough to measure the size of the smile he's sending me versus the one he was giving to her.

That's just ridiculous behavior.

I clear my throat, avoiding Sebastian, and look straight at Vera. "They are setting up inside the bookstore now. Maybe you want to freshen up?"

Vera nods. "Is Doris around?"

I point to the side where the makeup artist is waiting, and she turns to Sebastian. "I hope this is ok? The wind is cutting my skin, and I think Doris might have a lip balm."

Sebastian nods. "Of course. Go on."

Vera finally takes her hand off him, but Sebastian grabs it back and kisses it before she goes.

I won't gag.

Vera giggles like a schoolgirl, tucking a strand of her hair behind her ear, and races toward Dora.

Vera and Sebastian are the perfect couple. The fact slams into me like a ton of bricks. It's marketing genius, picture-perfect. They are the reason people watch reality TV.

I want to pull my hair out. I try to regulate my breathing because, after all, everything is going according to plan. I hate Sebastian so much right now.

I'm irritated he broke the rules and came to sit with me for almost eleven hours after I ignored him for weeks. I'm frustrated that those hours made me remember how much I missed him.

And now? I'm pissed he's not the same with Vera. I know this is what we wanted at the beginning, but now that I truly know him, the British robot won't cut it. I hate the Prince Charming persona who takes over when the cameras are rolling.

I want to scream in his face.

"Do you need a touch-up?" I ask without looking at him.

"Do you think I do?"

I raise my eyebrow but end up looking up at his ridiculously good-looking face. No. He looks perfect, but I shrug instead of complimenting him.

Sebastian's eyes narrow, and he steps closer. Out of instinct, I step back. His eyes flare, something powerful behind them. I face him because I'm not one to cower, but I can't deny I like how primal he looks right now.

Maybe we need to fight. I'd love to fight him right now.

I bury my hands in my battered jacket pockets and avert my eyes.

"You look upset."

"I'm cold," I reply quickly.

Sebastian tsks. "You were right, Calliope."

"Callie," I breathe. "I'm sure I was right, but about what?"

He nods in Vera's direction. "Vera is great. I'm glad I didn't eliminate her in the first week."

I grunt. "I'm a genius, Riggs. Listen, now it's the time for a bathroom break because–"

"And you know, it's hard to see what you really want in a person right away. I knew what I wanted to feel, but I did not know what this person would look like."

"Well, she looks like a drop-dead gorgeous princess with a very complicated job."

Isn't that kick-you-in-the-crotch-spit-on-your-neck fantastic? I add to myself in Rachel Green's voice.

He says nothing, so I boldly look up at his face. I'm in for a fight. I want to punish him for something. He doesn't reply, though. He reaches for his microphone and turns it off while smiling at me.

I frown at it, and he steps closer again, but this time, I keep my ground.

"We're meeting Bea tonight," he tells me.

"Your sister?"

Sebastian slowly nods. I'm already shaking my head, but he stops me. "She can escape for a couple of hours."

My throat feels dry, and I still say nothing. But Sebastian keeps talking. "Come on, Callie. You said you'd meet her. I rather think you'll love Bea."

"I'm sure she's great," I blurt out.

"So come out for a pint. Just one, even though coming out for one is simply not done."

I chuckle a little, rubbing my forehead and dislodging my beanie. I want to say no and end this conversation, but instead, I see myself asking: "Why are you so different on camera?"

He frowns.

"Why are you... I don't know..." I touch my earpiece, as if it can make me remember. "You're so--"

"That's a lot of tiptoeing around something you're dying to say."

"I can't say it's fake." I blink. "It's just something else. I can't see you when I hear him."

"Him being the Sebastian in front of the cameras?"

I nod, and he looks at me carefully. "You told me to tone it down."

I opened my mouth, but he kept going. "You said I needed media training. Remember that?"

"I know I said that," I reply, smoothing my jacket unnecessarily. "But now, I think the opposite."

"Oh, I see," he replies wryly.

I turn my chin up, not stopped by his mocking tone. "If you really want to connect and find a wife--"

Sebastian smiles, stepping closer to me again. "That's definitely why I'm here."

"So, you must be yourself. Then, Vera can fall in love."

I swallow the lump down my throat, and I feel bad for ever having said that. The image is nothing compared to the real deal.

It isn't fair to put Sebastian in a box he can't fit in. Not a man who is larger than life, with a presence that can take all the air out of a room.

"I thought you wanted this for real," I say to him finally.

"And I do."

"So, be yourself."

We look at each other for a beat. The wind doesn't annoy me anymore. The whispers from the rest of the crew don't even register.

"Meet me at eight down in the atrium."

After Vera's date, Sebastian brings Abby to a famous vegan restaurant, but I don't have it in me to follow them. I murmur to Anya I'm feeling sick, and since I never get sick, she lets me go, even though I know she doesn't trust a word I say.

In a way, I'm not lying. I *do* feel sick. My head is a mess, and I know I made a mistake.

Weeks ago, Anya asked me to keep my head in the game. I knew I was getting too close to Sebastian, so I stepped back.

But it made it worse. *Way* worse.

Sebastian became this candy bar I wasn't allowed to have. The prize after my run, the glass of wine after a stressful day. I wanted to speak with him, listen to him. Be with him.

I lay my head on the pillow every night, thinking about

how much I ached to talk to him, just to reprimand myself a second later.

It was torture, and even after all that, I was back to my old habits the second he sat beside me on that flight. No time had passed, no walls had been built.

Feeling like a failure, I sit on the bed looking at nothing.

I can't move.

I can't call and cancel, but I can't go either. In my head, I know it's not a big deal. I've been friends with other contestants before. I've offered my shoulder for girls to cry on. I still go for drinks with the season seven cast at least once a year.

I inhale deeply and tell myself that. I'm allowed to have friends. Sebastian is just a really hot friend. People have those. I have a bunch of those.

As I survey the clothes I brought with me, I remember that never in the history of my employment has Anya called me out like that. She never needed to ask me to keep my head in the game.

Annnd I'm back to overreacting.

I groan, feeling pathetic. I grab a *Metallica* tee and dark jeans. There. That's me. Tee, jeans, and boots. I refuse to dress up to meet his sister.

But Beatrice is a fancy name.

I bet my arm Sebastian's sister is the most gorgeous woman I've ever laid my eyes on.

I really want her to like me. She's escaping her mother's clutches just to meet little me.

So, I have no choice, really. I need to change. For Beatrice, of course. I grab the one dress I packed, black, but tight on my body, and it looks good paired with my boots, too.

I throw everything on and fix my hair to the best of my abilities, and before I start to rethink the whole ordeal, I go to the elevator without looking back.

It's just a drink.

One.

Just a quick hello and nice to meet you, so sorry you won't be on the show. Oh sure, it's a pleasure to see the girls throwing themselves at your brother.

Me? I'm peachy. I love this damn weather. It's doing wonders for my hair and complexion.

I close my eyes and step into the elevator, pressing the button for the atrium. My fingers drum over my legs with anxious energy, and I let go a long breath right when the doors click open, and I get the full vision of the man waiting for me

My body freezes as I take him in.

I falter. *Oh God!*

Sebastian awaits in a blue shirt that, by some magic, is the exact shade of his eyes. The first button is open over his neck, and the sleeves are folded three-quarters of the way. God, why are forearms so damn sexy? His are veiny and thick, with golden hair all over. And does it do it for me? Shit, yes, it does, big time.

The elevator door starts to close on me again, and he chooses that moment to look up from his phone. Our eyes lock, and I spring back to life, using my hand to stop the doors from closing.

This is a bad idea.

Because Sebastian looks like *that*. I do not know how the girls can walk toward him in heels every episode. I'm wearing my Doc Martens, and I'm walking like Bambi on ice.

I gulp. I can't look into his eyes. They are too damn beautiful. I can't look at his smile because his white teeth are blinding. I can't look at his forearms because they make me want to fall just to see if he'd catch me.

So, I look down.

This is ridiculous. Of all the times we put him on camera, nothing compares to this. He pockets his phone and turns his body to me, coming in my direction with strong and certain steps, watching me.

I clutch my bag, not trusting my knees anymore, and halt to a stop. He smirks when we are a foot away from each other, rubbing his chin as he looks me up and down.

"Darling, you look incredible."

Calliope Sosa would let no one call her *darling*. But the way Sebastian says it? I melt like an idiot.

He smiles like it's a secret, and I stand there, licking my bottom lip, no words coming out. Sebastian's hand tugs mine toward the doors, and I follow, knowing fully well how much trouble I'm in.

He calls a car and puts me in the back seat, sliding in after me. His smell, his voice, and his presence fill the backseat and raise the hair down my arm.

And that's when I know for sure I have a crush on the star.

CHAPTER 11
Sebastian

We got here a couple minutes early, just the right time to get a drink before I spot the strawberry blonde of my sister's head coming our way. She bounces over to us with a huge smile, dressed in a stripy jumper and black leggings. I love seeing her like this. No buttons, no matching sets or pearls.

Beatrice likes to be free, to tend to her horses, to talk to her friends about Taylor Swift. She's a normal girl of her age, and I wish she could always be like this.

I'm overtaken by Bea's hug. I squeeze her hard in return. My mother always tried her best to keep us in line and show a unified front. The four of us were always together at events, but since I strayed, she's been keeping Bea from me.

Since I broke the news of *The Final Rose*, I haven't seen Bea. Thankfully, Bea is so busy at uni, she's blissfully unaware of how dramatic Mum is being about the subject. Better like this. I don't want Bea getting caught in the crossfire. She can start her own revolution when she sees fit.

"Look at you! College kid," I joke.

She sways her palm over my chest. "Do I look properly broke and lost?" She makes a pose, and I approve.

Not that Beatrice Elizabeth Riggs will ever be broke, but I get what she means. She looks normal. And that's all the Riggs children ever wanted.

"Who do we have here?" Bea looks away from me with that beaming smile of hers. "The famous Callie!"

Callie seems to be taken aback, but my sister gives her no time to react. In a second, she's on the other woman, giving her the biggest hug.

"You're so pretty. Oh my God, Sebastian! You never told me she was so pretty!"

I clear my throat, because I'm sure I tell people everything about Callie all the time. But I can't look too long in her direction, not when she's dressed like a dream come true. Normally, I can't get enough of her shorts showing off her shapely legs, but then, she decides to kill me with that dress.

That dress. I need to swallow my groan.

"I can't believe you're not telling everyone how pretty I am, Riggs," Callie fires.

"I'm sure I said it." I arch an eyebrow and pull a chair for Bea.

"He said you're pretty," Bea agrees, taking a seat. "But you look like a movie star."

Callie snorts in a very non-movie-star way, and that just makes me want her even more. It's the way she looks, the shape of her body, and that insolent mouth of hers. It's all too alluring.

Shaking her head, Callie sips the cider I got her. "And I was scared you wouldn't like me."

Bea gasped. "Utter tosh! I'd love anyone who puts my brother in his place."

"Oh, that I do." Callie smiles coyly at me, and I can't even say something witty.

I need to get hold of myself, but it's hard.

She's gorgeous. It's easy like that. I always plan my days around her, but today, it took an uncomfortable turn. I can't banter because I can't look anywhere else but her tits. They look about to burst from that dress. The fabric fits her so perfectly, it leaves very little to the imagination.

I'm a tortured man.

I clear my throat and look to the safe side of the table, my sister. "What do you fancy, Bea?"

Bea makes a little face, looking away from Callie to check the beer taps over the bar. "Anything that looks nice."

"How old are you?" Callie asks.

"Nineteen."

Callie breathes out, "Gotta love Europe."

"Proper fun over here," I agree, and she rolls her eyes.

Once we all have drinks, Bea goes to the jugular. "So, tell me, how's the show going?"

Callie sips. "Are you asking me about the six women your brother is currently dating?"

Bea wriggles her nose. "Ew. I didn't think about it that way. Gross, Sebastian, why are you dating six women?"

I rub my face. I should know better to get these two together. "I'm not exactly dating–"

"Oh, I think that's exactly what you are doing," Callie insists.

"So, you like cider?" I try to change the subject, but all she gives me is a half-shrug with an innocent smile.

"Can you tell me anything about the girls?" Bea asks. "Or it's super against the contract?"

"Super against the contract," Callie confirms before I do. "But I can say they are all extremely beautiful, and I'm sure Sebastian's wife is one of them."

She's looking straight at me when she says it. They are her words, but they leave a bitter taste on my tongue.

"Is that true? Are you falling in love?" Bea pokes.

And I don't even think about it. I eye Callie and say, "Yes."

"Tell me about your classes," I ask when Callie excuses herself to the loo.

Bea rolls her eyes. "Who cares? Let's talk about Callie."

I drink so I can avoid my sister's gaze. Three pints in, I don't trust myself to keep the charade. Bea arches her eyebrow every time Callie says something about me or when we laugh together. They became fast friends like I thought they would, but I know what she's trying to get from me.

"Yes, Callie is great," I say, just to let the subject go.

"It's Callie."

"Excuse me?"

"It's Callie," she repeats, putting her pint down so she can brace the table. "It's Callie."

"I heard just fine the second time, but Bea..."

"Callie is the one for you, Seb. I didn't even meet the other girls, but I don't think it's necessary."

"Bea, listen. Yes, we get along well, but--"

"Oh, don't you start with the Riggs bullshit!" She waves me off. "I want the dirt, Seb. Tell me."

I give one more look to where Callie disappeared and then face my sister. "Can you imagine the consequences? I signed a contract, Bea."

"Ah-ha!" she screams, pointing a finger at me.

"Don't point your dirty finger at me, Beatrice," I say, slapping it away.

I hold no respect, and my baby sister simply laughs. "So, you like Callie."

It went straight up my spine. "And Callie loves her job."

Bea pouts. "This is so romantic, Seb. You falling for her is much better than anything I could think of. There's no way around it?"

"It's not like I have to marry one of the girls. But I can't date Callie."

And for the first time, I say what is bugging me, the words I wouldn't dare to say even when I was alone. "I'd ruin her career. She loves her job. She's bloody excellent at it."

"Love that you curse now."

"Oh, thank you. Arsehole is another one I'm quite fond of."

"Lovely use of language. Mother would be proud."

I chuckle, and Bea follows. Shaking my head, I take a sip, looking around the pub. I remember when I wanted to go out for drinks, but my parents were always thinking about the press. They were scared I was going to be seen drinking, and people would say all kinds of things about me.

Saying that a Riggs was off the rails.

Now, it seems so far away, so stupid of me to ever believe their opinion mattered.

"You know everything our parents say is a lie, right?"

Bea's eyebrow shoots up. "Oh, well, wild change of subject."

I nod, agreeing, but I keep it up. "They are obsessed with how things look. But nothing will ever make them happy, so just be you. You know that, right?"

Bea tilts her head and reaches for my hand across the table. "Seb, you are the oldest. Their only son. Yes, Mum loves me in pearls and soft colors, but they don't put that much pressure on me. Just maybe marry well."

"Oh God," I groan. "Marry whoever you want. *If* you want."

"I know." She laughs. "I saw what they did to you, Seb. All

the impossible standards. I hate them for that, and I'm glad you broke free."

I take a sip from my pint. "Bloody hell." I rake my hand through my hair. "Getting drunk and emotional, are we?"

"You're just a pub commoner now." She straightens up again, with a glint in her eyes. Across the pub, I catch Callie coming back from the bathroom, and Bea rushes to say. "Now that you're free, don't let anyone tell you what you're supposed to do, Seb. It's Callie. I'm telling you. It's Callie."

I give the hotel's address to the driver as soon as I'm in. Callie is by my side, red cheeks from the alcohol. I sent Bea in another car after she gave us both a warm hug and a suggestive nod toward Callie.

I can't think about Bea's words right now. I have too many pints in me, and while I'm not exactly drunk, I'm feeling too light and free. Nothing good comes from this lightness of spirit. Callie moves beside me, dropping her jacket off her shoulders.

"Is that the trick?" she asks when the car presses forward. "Drink until you're not cold anymore?"

I laugh because she's not wrong, but the laughter falls dead in my throat when she wiggles free of her jacket. Her tits shake inside that dress, and my vision blurs.

We should have gone somewhere for tea instead. Somewhere with florals and old ladies. Without alcohol.

"I loved Bea." Callie beams. "She's the best."

I clear my throat and look away. "I told you you'd get on just fine."

I feel her nodding. "Still, she's a Riggs. I thought she was going to be all fancy. But she's a normal kid, isn't she?"

I face back at her. "She's a good one."

Callie nods and rests her body on the seat as she rolls her head to face me. "Thank you for introducing me to her."

"Thank you for coming. For a second there, I thought you wouldn't."

I almost curse myself when I let that slip out. I'm ready to move along and not get too serious, but Callie nods, biting her lip.

"I thought about it," she confesses.

I swallow a lump. "Why?" She shrugs, but now, I'm a dog with a bone. "Why do you avoid me so much?"

Her lips part, her eyes tracing my face with a lazy disposition.

I come closer, and her breathing hitches. Taking it to the next level, I touch her knee. Her skin is warm, despite the cold outside. I want to groan when I trace her soft skin with the pad of my fingers.

"Why would you keep yourself away from me?" I push my hand, traveling further.

"Sebastian." She says my name in a way that unravels me.

"I have a few theories. I might be wrong. You should just tell me."

Her lips part as my hand travels up her thigh, taking it all in my palm, under her dress, my thumb drawing circles inside her leg.

"You should never make assumptions," she says in a breathy voice. I can't wait to hear more.

"So, you agree telling me is the best option?" I can't stop myself from smirking.

Callie's skin is soft and sun-kissed. My hand reaches the end of its journey, my thumb grazes lace, and Callie hums. I know I'm too far gone to back down now.

With my other hand, I grip the back of her neck. Gathering her soft hair in my hands, I slide her closer to me. My thumb finds home between her legs, and her mouth opens in a gasp.

The streets of London race out the dark windows. Her huge, bottomless brown eyes are all I see and, in a blink, I'm kissing her.

My mouth takes hers. Her lips are soft under mine, her taste addictive. I feel the warmth of Callie's hands as she clutches my shirt. She raises her head from the backrest and, in a second, she kisses me as much as I'm kissing her.

Her tongue works against mine like nothing else, her chest so close, I know she's not wearing a bra. I'm lifting her leg, four fingers around her ass, and she whimpers in my mouth.

I lick down her throat and up her earlobe. Her hands are frantic, just like I feel. This kiss can never end. I'm back to her mouth. She digs her teeth into my bottom lip, and my whole body shakes. The noises I make aren't even human.

It was never like this. Never. I need to get her naked and under me. My mind is on track. Callie. Her soft body under mine, her voice on my ear, her legs around my waist.

The car stops. The driver clears his throat, and with force, Callie stops the kiss.

We move apart. I look down at my legs, trying to regain control.

"Cheers, mate." I barely finish saying it to the driver when I feel the gush of cold wind and hear the slam of a door.

Callie's gone.

Isla holds her tongue and turns to me, making a face. She's a soft-spoken, petite yoga instructor, but previously on a group date, she told me how much she loved horror films and books, so of course, I brought her on the Jack the Ripper walking tour.

The production had to pull a few strings to get the tour filmed and tourists agreeing to be part of it, but they pulled it off, and I'm honestly impressed with my choice.

What did not impress me was the lack of Callie Sosa.

The woman is nowhere to be found since the morning shooting. I went to Warner Bros Studios with Maya, the Harry Potter fan, then I took Grace to a traditional afternoon tea. Now, I'm following Jack the Ripper's steps around London, but Callie vanished into thin air.

I have to concentrate extra hard to make the basics of conversation; I want to feel bad, but my brain is mush.

The only thing I can think of is Callie's taste in my mouth and the little whimper she let go when I kissed her.

I only have one more date tomorrow morning, a walk in the park with Mackenzie. At first, I wanted Hyde Park, but they didn't clear it for production, so we changed to Victoria Park. It's all good to me. Talking to Mackenzie is the challenge, not our location. I already know I'm going to eliminate her next, but then again...

I know I'm going to eliminate all of them.

I take a deep breath of the cold London air. Isla smiles at me, buried in her beanie with the cutest red nose from the cold.

I will eliminate Isla and her sweet contradictions.

And Maya, with the nerdiness, Grace, and her southern charm. Abby, the foodie, and Vera, who is, without any doubt, the perfect woman.

Yet, I'll eliminate them all because I can't think about anyone but the producer of *The Final Rose*. I want to say last night was a surprise, but I can't fool myself like that. That kiss was bound to happen ever since I laid my eyes on her.

She's mine.

I can't pinpoint when I realized it, but here we are. I scan the crowd once more. People gather around us, trying to figure out what is being filmed while the crew holds them off.

Callie is nowhere.

I tune back to Isla, engaging with what she's saying. The night is full of stars, and Isla is holding onto my arm like a lifeline.

"Do you ever walk around here and be like, *oh, people were murdered right here?*"

"I'm sorry, my dear, but I think we can say that about most streets."

Isla giggles too loudly. I widen my eyes, and she claps her hand over her mouth. Next, she's whispering, conscious of the tour guide still talking at the front. "I know, but these are famous murders."

"You're right, these are posh murders."

"...The kidney was delivered to the police as a taunt from the killer..." the guide is saying.

"Maybe regular murders are better after all," Isla concludes, making me chuckle.

She was an easy one to talk to. Great sense of humor just on the edge of weirdness. If I took anything from *The Final Rose*, it's that they are real, genuine people.

I don't know if I fully understood before, even when I signed up for the show, but as I laugh about something else that Isla is saying, it hits me.

Isla is here to fall in love.

And a month ago, I'd be giving everything in me to engage and make this the best date ever. But now?

I feel almost sad about the way she looks at me.

By the end of the date, I know Isla is one of my favorite

people I have gotten to meet. We are bent over the waist, laughing at something inappropriate, when she sobers up, turning to me. "You're the real deal, right?"

My mouth dries up, and I face her. She's small in my arms, looking up at me with big, trusting eyes. And I want to say I am the real deal, because I entered with all good intentions. But I'm not that man anymore.

"I believe in love," I reply instead.

She takes her arm from mine, facing me completely. She looks too deep, and I'm nervous for a second.

"Me too," Isla says. "But I also think love takes you by surprise and sweeps you off your feet. So, I'm going to propose something here, Sebastian."

I lick my lips, my eyes flying to the cameras too close to us. I can't let myself forget about them.

"What do you propose?"

"Kiss me," she says, lifting her chin.

I take a second to reply, but she's already talking again. "And then we'll know. If there's anything here..." She takes a big breath and lets the rest of the sentence linger.

My lips still taste like Callie, and I want it to stay like that for a little longer. But Isla is asking for so little. She came looking for love, for the perfect connection, and if it was this that I was looking for, I'd kiss her without a thought.

I realize I can't tell her no. This is the proof she wants for the connection, and for all it's worth, I don't have a good excuse to refuse.

I say nothing. Instead, I lower down, and Isla takes the hint and goes up on her tiptoes. I don't take her mouth in mine the way I did Callie. I don't feel the warmth of her lips everywhere.

I kiss her gently, respectfully, sending a message. When we open our eyes to each other, I know Isla sees it. She looks disappointed, but the look only flits for a second on her face.

She lifts her shoulder, almost as if she's telling herself it's alright.

I think of the cameras and how they are pointing at us, waiting for words to be the next episode's tagline. Isla and I don't give it to them. We watch each other in silent conversation, coming to an agreement of sorts.

Isla's eyes shine in the streetlights when she looks up at me, a green so vivid, I'm not sure how I didn't realize it until now.

"I believe in love, Sebastian. I believe in right on your face, chemistry off the charts, romance novel kind of love."

"Me too."

We smile at each other like it's the perfect ending to a date.

I eliminate Isla the next day.

CHAPTER 12

Callie

My fingers hover over the keyboard, but my eyes never leave the screen.

Rewind.

"I believe in love, Sebastian. I believe in right on your face, chemistry off the charts, romance novel kind of love."

I blink, Isla's statement going through my skull like a sledgehammer. The girl is a fairy-looking thing. Even though we're of similar height, she has something delicate and undeniably cute about her.

I should think how annoying it's going to be to pull all of Isla's footage to make this change of storyline make sense. I know we can do it, but we need to sit down and redirect our team. I should have rolled my eyes at such a line, but instead...

Instead, I'm frozen in place, my fingers on the keyboard, rewinding, watching the kiss over and over again.

It's a sweet type of kiss. Perfect for Prince Charming and his princess.

Not the hot mess, tongues, hands everywhere while an Uber driver witnesses it. Those kinds of kisses are for messy girls like me.

I squeeze my eyes shut. I can't stand here and feel sorry for myself. I was drunk; he was drunk. We got caught up in the moment, and I need to get my head back in the game. That was why I volunteered to arrive at the country house beforehand with part of the crew.

I ignore that it's his house I'm escaping to. His country, his domain.

As much as the house isn't the warm home of childhood, I can't stop myself from seeing him everywhere. And now, I can't stop watching the footage of him kissing Isla.

On repeat. Again and again. Her hands went up his chest, his face bowing down to her. The beat that followed the kiss, like goddamn wonder.

"Oh, have you seen this?"

A chuckle took me from my insanity, and I turned to find Dave, one of our tech guys, with a cigarette on the back of his ear.

"Yeah. Crazy stuff," I say mildly, crossing my arms in front of my chest, hoping he wouldn't see how much I was shaking.

Dave barks a laugh, coughing right after. I tsk, tilting my head right. "Dave, you told me you were going to quit."

Dave waves me off. "Anya is arriving soon. You better meet her quickly. She's angry."

I chance to look back at the screen, regretting straight away when it's Sebastian's impossible blues frozen and staring at me. I gulp and turn to Dave. "Is she upset he's not going for Vera?"

Dave's eyebrows disappear through his hairline. "Because he eliminated her."

My spine went straight. "Vera?"

I never miss an elimination. I left a very unhappy Anya in London, but I convinced myself it was for the best. How did things get so crazy in so little time?

Twenty-four hours ago, his lips were on mine. Twenty-four hours ago, Vera and Abby were in the lead, and the only hiccup we had was trying to convince him not to eliminate Mackenzie too quickly.

How the hell in twenty-four hours did he decide to spare Mackenzie and go for Vera?

"Kid." Dave shakes his head, taking me back to the moment. "He eliminated Isla."

I'm marching out of the room before I even understand where my feet are taking me. I pound the perfect wooden floors and stare at the front, ignoring the elegant floral wallpaper and the arched doorways.

Fuming, I'm almost outside when my radio beeps, and I hear Anya's voice saying only one word: *"Callie."*

Of course, it's my name she calls the second I'm in range. I open the front door as the headlights of three cars come to the front lawn gravel. I turn my radio off as Anya exits the first car; her face looks murderous.

"Did you know?"

"Dave told me just now," I reply, ignoring the insinuation that I'd know about Sebastian's plans.

"He keeps changing the script." Anya heads to the house, and I follow her steps. "The elimination came from nowhere. His date with Mackenzie was terrible. I knew while it was happening we had no way to keep her. Not without making him look like a jerk."

She curses in Polish under her breath. After years of working under Anya, I know enough Polish to understand none of the words she just used are pretty. The double doors open like she's Moses, and then, we are in the house. The crew respects Anya. They know even though Jeff is the director and Adam the showrunner, Anya is the shark you should fear.

Executives trust her to bring the money, make the season profitable, and keep the lights on. The respect of the crew, she earned because she never stops. This is her world, and we all know how to read her expressions at this point.

Tonight, the ferocity in her eyes and the set of her jaw make my hands tremble.

We move to the back of the house, to the small office I left minutes ago, but Dave is nowhere to be found. Smart man. But the footage of Isla and Sebastian is still on pause on screen, and I have to move my eyes to the floral walls to avoid looking at his lips on her.

"*This* I can handle." Anya points to the screen. "Eligibles going off script, contestants becoming a favorite suddenly."

"He eliminated Isla," I say in my calming voice. "So, we are back to Vera." There has to be an upside to this.

Anya brings her hand to her waist. "We'll need to chop his date with Mackenzie to death because I can't justify keeping her."

I'm about to ask if it's that bad, but the usual players arrive, silencing me. Jeff, Devi, and then Adam, followed by Nessa. With a soft click, Nessa closes the door.

Adam watches Anya with an arched brow. "It's not that bad."

Another Polish curse. It's one of those days.

"I don't like to be scrambling around. I don't like improvising."

"It's reality TV," Devi makes the mistake of pointing out.

The look Anya spares him burns even me on the other side of the room.

"Can someone explain to me what happened out there?" I ask, massaging my temple.

"Well, you haven't explained why you needed to be here earlier than everyone else," Anya fires back, pointing her finger at me."

"I wanted to–"

Thank God Adam interrupts me, trying to keep us on the right track. "Sebastian and Mackenzie had a horrible date.

There wasn't a way to salvage it. She's a difficult person to edit."

Jeff snorts. "She's a self-obsessed bitch," he offers. "And Sebastian wasn't hiding how much he dislikes her."

"As much as I'd like to keep her for the drama..." Adam shakes his head. "After that date, it would hurt Sebastian's image."

"She made comments about politics." Nessa wrinkles her nose.

My eyebrows rise. So it's *that* bad. I should have watched their date, but I was too annoyed at Sebastian, and I hate Mackenzie's guts.

Nessa bobs her head. "Oh yeah, it's bad. Everything she said was at the same time misinformed, confused, and just plain...." She swallows something that was on the tip of her tongue. It's bad."

"It was tough to watch," Adam concedes. "But it was ok. Sebastian has wanted her gone for weeks now, and we were finally on the same page until..." He trails off and looks at the screen.

Until Sebastian kissed Isla. And eliminated her right after.

I swallow the lump in my throat, refusing to be anything but professional. This nonsense already hurt me enough. They never had to update me on events. I'm always there with them. But today, of all days, I decided to wake up at the crack of dawn and head with the set crew to the country with a flimsy excuse.

"So then we have to change the fucking narrative so Isla is the main girl," Anya explains, as if it's needed. "Which is fine... But then he goes and..." She waves at nothing, trailing off.

"Did they have a good date before..." I clear my throat.

"It was cute," Nessa offers. "She's a nice girl. She might just be a little camera shy, so she didn't exactly shine."

"She's a season filler," Anya interrupts. "Nice enough, but

a complete season filler, and we all need to take footage out of our asses to make this make sense."

"We have footage of them all," Jeff starts. "We did it before and we'll do it again. You just hate when people don't behave like your puppets, Anya."

"And what about the elimination, uh?" she challenges. "It's a kiss, and then he sends her home? How can we make this ok? People are going to hate him."

"We don't need to show the kiss," Adam ponders. "If we limited the date to something with little spark. We don't need to act like this is a big deal."

"Remember season six when Mark and Caroline got together off camera, and we needed to explain why he was choosing her?" Jeff laughs. "Anya went crazy."

"Well, shit for brains, this job isn't just filming it. We need to make the public buy the story. We need them to like the outcome. And how can we do this when this shithead goes off the rails?"

"He's not off the rails, Anya–" Adam shakes his head, but it's Nessa who interrupts.

"I think he eliminated Isla because she asked."

We all look at her like she grew a second head or started talking with an English accent. Twisting her mouth, Nessa goes to the screen, rewinding the raw footage I was just using for self-harm.

We're silent while watching the last words they shared after the kiss. My hands close in a fist, my nails digging into my palm, but I have no reaction besides that.

"See?" Nessa says when the clip ends. "She wanted a kiss to see if they were compatible. And then she says she believes in a fierce kind of love." Nessa goes to the clip again, stopping on Isla's close-up after the kiss. "This is not the face of a woman who was just kissed by someone she cares about."

"Oh," Anya scoffs. "And now we are here, analyzing their faces and–"

"What I am saying, Anya," Nessa continues over gritted teeth, "is that you're so afraid of what the public will think about this elimination, but this makes Sebastian the ultimate good guy."

There's a pause, and then Adam is nodding. "The exit interview. We can get Isla to confirm this version of the story on camera, and we do the same when Sebastian arrives."

Everyone agrees, and Anya looks straight at me. "Go back to London and get that exit interview. I'd let Kara deal with it, but if it's this important, I need *you* to talk to Isla."

I open my mouth, not even sure why, but Anya is talking again. "If this isn't the story? Make it be. Make her say she's happy to be eliminated. Put Sebastian on a pedestal, you hear me?"

I'm only able to nod.

I should be happy to be in a car back to London. It isn't just that Anya trusts me to run things in her absence, but I wanted to avoid Sebastian, and there's nothing better than going in the opposite direction than he's heading, right?

It will delay our meeting by at least half a day. If I play my cards right, a full day.

I should be grateful, but instead, I'm wiggling my hands on top of my lap as the pastures of the English countryside run through the window.

The last thing I want is to have a lovely sit down with Isla and talk about the kiss. Whatever Nessa's theory is, the reality is that Sebastian kissed Isla.

That's that.

I'm being brought to the hotel where they filmed the elimination ceremony. Although it would be easier if we used the country house as the only and main location for our time in England, it made sense to the game to bring only the top five to his house.

I breathe through my nose and make a mental list of why this is the worst idea.

Sebastian has to be with one of the five girls. It's just a fact. He doesn't need to marry her, but he needs to be in a relationship for this to ring true.

We had couples before who didn't last a week after production wrapped up, but I thought Sebastian was different.

He said he was here for love, and I believed him. And idiotically, I still do. After meeting his sister, it was confirmed what he said. His family was always in the public eye. His parents raised him and Bea to be the perfect children. Every encounter he had with women was calculated and planned.

The Final Rose is his rebellion. Sure, many people will think he's full of it, but Sebastian really thinks this is his only way to meet someone.

I recline my head on the backrest of the passenger seat and take a calming breath. I want to be angry at Sebastian for kissing Isla right after kissing me. In a way, I'm very much so. But this thing was already a mess.

Sebastian and I crossed a line, and we were in the wrong. Him kissing one of the contestants is right. That should be a sign my future isn't completely lost. I just have to be smart about it.

I'm ready for a promotion, and I thought this season, I was going to prove to everyone I can do more. Get a bigger salary, take the project of Mom and Dad's new home off the ground, and hopefully, start planning for my own house.

That's the plan. That has always been the plan.
And yet...Sebastian Riggs.

"I'm so happy you're here!" Isla jumps on me, and we hug.

I arrive back in London late. Kara then tells me Isla's interview is scheduled first thing the next morning. So here I am, in the most horrible first hours of the morning, being jumped by Isla when my coffee isn't even ready. I asked an assistant to fetch me a cup, but he's still not back yet.

"I thought I was going to go before saying goodbye. They told me you were in the country house already."

"I was," I agree, tapping awkwardly on her back until she releases me. "But it was better for me to, you know..." I clear my throat.

It was better for me, of all people, to come here so we could talk about that time you kissed my man.

Not my man. Sebastian Fucking Riggs.

Isla folds her arms over her chest and makes a face. She watches me so intently, I feel like she watched my kiss with Sebastian too. I shake my head, feeling stupid.

"We need to talk about the unexpected elimination." I turn the conversation back to work and point to the chair in the middle of the room.

I take my spot beside the director's chair, today filled by Jeff's second assistant. This is the last thing we need to film, so of course, all the main crew is preparing for our next location. An exit interview should be simple, but suddenly, we are balancing an entire season on it.

Nick, the assistant, is back with my black coffee, and I

almost kiss him in gratitude. It's horribly weak, but this is England, and I take what I can get.

"I wouldn't think it's so unexpected. I wasn't a favorite, Callie."

I sip my coffee and rein in my grimace as the cameras turn on. I can't waste this conversation off-camera.

Andrew gives me a thumbs up, and I nod to Isla, letting her know she's being filmed now. I massage my temple, putting my head back in the game. As much as I'd love to know why Isla felt she wasn't a favorite, this isn't about that.

This is about the damn kiss.

I clear my throat and think about management control. "What do you think of the elimination?"

I start with the regular questions.

Isla smiles big. "I think Sebastian and I weren't meant to be. I'm still looking for my Prince Charming."

"But after the kiss, aren't you surprised he eliminated you?"

Isla is still smiling. Maybe Nessa's theory has something to it, because she's looking too happy for someone who just got dumped.

"Sebastian eliminated me because he knew it wasn't meant to be."

Great, we got into it quickly enough. "Can you just tell us about the date?"

"Or you just want to know about the kiss?" She tilts her head to the side, wiggling her eyebrows.

"That would be nice." I can't help but chuckle.

Isla readjusts on the chair, rolling her shoulder back, and it's story time. "I'm a romantic, and I like the idea of getting to know someone before the first kiss. But I also think a first kiss can say a lot about a couple. Compatibility, passion. I came here because I wanted to find someone who completed me, mind and body. Sebastian is amazing. He's handsome, funny, a total dreamboat!" She giggles. "But I wanted to feel the ulti-mate spark. That punch in the gut, you know?"

I nod, because what else can I do?

"Tingling sensation." As Isla talks, her eyes lose focus. "I wanted to be surprised, and I needed to know it for sure."

I wait a couple of seconds until I'm allowed to talk again so I don't mess up the editing, but even when I can talk, I'm not sure what to say.

"So, you don't think the kiss was all that?" I manage to ask.

Isla sighs. "I knew Sebastian wasn't for me. But I really wanted him to be, you know? A handsome man who is looking for love. Why not me? Why couldn't I be the one for him? But the thing is, we don't choose."

I must have made a face, because she rushed to keep talk-ing. "I couldn't make myself be the girl he was going to notice. And he couldn't make my heart beat faster."

I take a breath. "So, when you asked him to kiss you?"

"I asked him to kiss me so we'd know for sure it wasn't it. Sebastian knew I was underwhelmed, and he knew I was ready to love. He's a great guy like that." She shrugs. "He released me to the wild, I guess. But I'm grateful for this opportunity. I got to travel, and I know myself better than I knew months ago. And you know, now I have a friend who is practically English royalty."

She chuckles, and a few people follow. Even when they should be quiet on the set, I understand how captivating Isla can be. She's the best friend you never knew you needed, the nicest girl around.

"And you're going home because you deserve to find true love?"

"I deserve to find true love," Isla agrees. "But Sebastian deserves it too. He needs to find someone who he can't take his eyes off of."

And she winks at me.

CHAPTER 13

Sebastian

"Oh, you definitely got more handsome since you became the most eligible bachelor in America."

The familiar taunting makes me open a big smile as I go down the stairs to find Maverick right in the middle of the crew's mess.

"I've always been the most eligible bachelor," I reply.

He laughs, throwing his head up in that way he did since we were kids. The sight calms me. I can't stop thinking about Callie, and she's, again, missing. I was sure I was going to see her again once I left London, but Callie is avoiding me, and she's good at it.

Maverick gives me a half hug, patting me on the back. His smile is ridiculously big, and it hits me how much I need this right now. Bea was great, but there are twelve years between us, and for most of my life, I tried to protect her. Now that she's an adult, I'm excited to get to know her and build a relationship away from our parents, but as it is, it's no rival to my relationship with Maverick.

He knows my family well, even though Mother didn't think it was seemly to keep him as a friend. He saw hurt, but he chose to smile every single day. He knows me so well that after only a glimpse, a frown comes to his forehead.

"What's going on?"

I turn around, and like every day of *The Final Rose*, there's crew walking in all directions, talking loudly and making it impossible to have a private conversation.

As much as I'm used to their comings and goings, I can't talk about any of my doubts without being overheard.

"Let's go for a ride." I nod toward the door.

"A ride?" Maverick makes a face.

"Come on, you can't possibly forget how to horseback ride."

He scoffs, finally moving on his feet, but not before murmuring, "Oh, my bollocks."

As I imagined, Maverick knows how to ride, if I'm to ignore all the complaining he's determined to do. By the time we reach the back of the property on our horses, where no crew risked going yet, I heard all I never wanted to know about his *Crown Jewels*.

"Callie," I interrupt another long-winded sentence about his balls. "The producer."

"Oh, yes. Tell me about young Callie."

"We kissed." As I say out loud, I almost doubt if it really happened. I was drunk. It was quick, and she left me even quicker.

"And I'm only asking because I like to be meticulous, you know? But Callie is not a contestant?"

"No. Callie is the producer." I take a deep breath and trot the horse.

Maverick's horse follows the pace I set. "You're not supposed to kiss the producers, mate. It isn't an all-you-can-eat buffet over here."

"I swear, I'll shred your balls, Maverick–"

"Little Star here is already going for it. Don't worry." He

moves, unstable on the back of the poor horse, but finally sobers up. "Tell me exactly what happened."

I try to be clinical about it, so I tell him the events, the facts.

Fact: I brought Callie to meet Bea.

Fact: We were drunk.

Fact: We kissed, and she has yet to talk to me about it.

And of all the threads I thought Maverick was going to follow, once more, he surprises me. "Why did you invite Callie to meet Bea?"

I frown at him, looking back, but face ahead quickly. "I thought they would get on."

He chuckles. "That house is crawling with a crew. You've been dating twelve women at the same time for the last several–"

"People should stop saying I'm dating them all. It's not like that."

"It's exactly like that. You have a little group situation going on. You're friendly with many people, aren't you?"

I roll my shoulders back. "I'm a charismatic man."

"Oh, I'm sure you're extra charming with her."

I slice him a look that, of course, infuses no heat. "Mate, you liked her way before the kiss." He finally reaches his point. "You brought her to meet your family. I think I brought Fael home after a year together. Mostly because I felt bad to subject them to him."

"You introduced me to Fael on your third date," I kindly remind him. "It was a very awkward affair."

"Oh, well, it's better to keep them on their toes."

I can't start going through Maverick's attempts to keep his husband on his toes, so I'm silent for a bit.

The horses go around the property in a rehearsed fashion, and while I only suggested the ride to be away from wandering ears, I'm happy we got out.

My favorite childhood memories happened on these grounds. Whether my mother and father were with us or not, I always spent the entire duration of the summer holidays in this house. I loved it so much, my father gave it to me for my eighteenth birthday. At first, I thought it was a silly present. The house was in the family anyway. There was no reason to attach my name to it. But now, with my forced removal from the Riggs, I'm glad the only thing I loved about that life is intact.

"How is she ignoring you?"

I come back to myself with Maverick's voice. "Not ignoring. Avoiding. She left London to come here, but now, I have no idea where she is."

"Do you think she's back in the States?"

I turn to him quickly, a frown on my forehead. "I didn't even consider that."

Maverick whistles. "That's what I would do if my job was hanging by a thread."

Another blow I didn't see coming. "Her job isn't hanging by a thread," I say firmly.

"Sebastian." The way he says my name irritates me to no end.

The good thing about old friends is that they know you. The bad thing about old friends is that *they fucking know you.*

"This has nothing to do with her job," I try again.

"Ok, sure, let's be delusional for a hot second here," he says theatrically. "What exactly are you planning to say to her?"

"When I see her?"

He only makes a gesture with his hand so I can go ahead.

Trying not to look in his direction, I start. "I'm going to ask her what she thought about the kiss."

"Sure, a survey is always important."

"Maverick..." I start.

"Sorry, go on."

"And then I will let my feelings known."

"Your feelings?"

"That I'm thrilled about the kiss."

"A lovely lukewarm feeling."

I throw my hands in the air. "What exactly do you want from me? We only kissed once!"

"Hey, I'm not trying to attack you here, but it's a kiss that shouldn't have ever happened. It's a kiss that can jeopardize her work–"

I open my mouth to disagree, but he's ahead of me, raising a palm before I even let a word out. "You can look at this at any angle, Sebastian, but it comes back to her work. You signed a contract to finish this season. She's one of the people who is here to make sure you fall in love with another woman."

I stop my horse, facing him with an edge to my jaw. "Are you saying it's doomed?"

"Not even I am that dramatic." He arches an eyebrow. "But maybe it's good she isn't here. You need to cool off and think about the consequences. I'm the first to say fuck the consequences, mate, but don't go off on a lukewarm feeling, huh?"

Maverick's words eat me up.

They follow me as I bring the horses back to the stables, as I take a shower and get ready for bed. This is our only day off between segments. The girls arrived, tucked in another side of the house. While many crew sleep here, many more are in the hotel close to our address.

I asked Maverick to arrive early because I thought it would be nice to have a day before a camera is mounted on our faces. But after the ride, my mood plummeted. Maverick feels the change, but in the true Maverick fashion, doesn't apologize for his words.

There's nothing to be sorry about, anyway. He's right. I signed up for this. I have a contract with *The Final Rose,* and they have a job to do. I can't simply walk away after a kiss with the producer.

I'll need to select one of the girls. I'll need to stay put and have more dates with each one of them and then announce my winner.

First, I think strategically. I can select one of them, end my contract, and break up straight away. I convince myself of that plan for about half an hour until it unravels in front of my eyes.

I care about them. They are kind and real. They are here because they believe we can build something together, and I can't say yes one day and dump them the next. It's just not right.

Not when the last episode usually announces the winner and the couple always shares a kiss.

For this to work, I'd need to tell them it's only for the show. But unfortunately, I can't trust any of them. They are nice enough, but this secret isn't just mine. I have Callie to think about.

The second hiccup of my plan is the fact that Callie will be still employed by the network even once my season is finished.

I can't date her without them knowing.

It's the middle of the night, and I'm in bed with an arm over my face, but ever so awake. I was so wrapped up in the kiss, I didn't think about what this really meant.

There's no way around it. Not if I want to protect Callie.

Of course, I don't want to break the contract or hurt the girls, but it's all about Callie for me.

By half past two, I'm thinking, how long did she know? When we got so close in the first weeks and everything came into a perfect lock, she stepped away. It was too early in the game for me to put a finger on it, but Callie built a wall between us, and as much as I tried, until the flight over, I couldn't get past it.

She knew it.

She knew if given time, we would get involved. If given the opportunity, we'd kiss.

Something stirs inside of me, and I'm on my feet. A hot curl at the base of my spine spreads. I let out a growl from the back of my throat. I've been working on reasons why I shouldn't ever touch her, but knowing she felt this pull from the beginning is doing serious things to me.

I race downstairs in search of water. In an hour, I know the crew will start setting up, always an ungodly early start. But I can't think that far ahead.

My head is with her, in our kiss, and the doomed feeling flees, replaced by something stronger.

I reach the kitchen and open the fridge for a bottle of water. I'm draining the bottle when the back door opens, and I hear a gasp.

She doesn't have time to retreat. I turn my head quickly, catching Callie coming in with a ridiculous amount covering her: jacket, scarf, hat, you name it. I drop the bottle on the marble island and advance on her. I see her gulping and widening her eyes. She steps back.

"What were you doing out there?"

"Couldn't sleep."

"Close the door. You're letting the heat out."

She blows a breath like I'm the biggest inconvenience of her life, and I can't even blame her.

As she latches the door closed, I step closer. When she turns, I'm stalking her.

"Go to sleep, Sebastian."

I ignore her request. "Where did you go?"

"I was working," she tells me, looking down and stepping to the side to evade me.

I follow her and press. "I thought I was your job."

Her eyes blast to mine, giving me the reaction I wanted. I'm a bastard for wanting a reaction from her, but I'm standing here trembling to touch her. My hands close in a fist because I don't trust myself.

"I had to go back to London to conduct the interview about why you would kiss a girl and eliminate her the next day."

I wince. The look she throws at me is fire. It almost burns. "I couldn't refuse her, Callie."

"I don't understand why you eliminated her," she says back and tries again to circle me.

"Callie, that's not wh–"

"Don't say another word, Sebastian!" She points a finger at me. "You were never even close to Isla, and then you kiss her and eliminate her right after? Did you ever consider what that looks like?"

The hollow laugh coming off my lips is impossible to hold off. "What would it look like? I thought you wanted to find me a wife! I thought this was genuine."

"It is!" she whisper-shouts, frustrated. "It doesn't mean it's not a televised show."

"Fuck TV, Callie."

"Shut up and go to sleep." This time, she pushes me away. I almost let her go, but at the last minute, my hand finds her wrist.

"Is that why you're angry? Because I eliminated Isla?"

"Yes," she spits through her gritted teeth.

"And what you wanted was for me to choose her, is that it? Kiss her longer? Give you a true Hollywood ending?"

"Go fuck yourself, Sebastian."

"I want to hear it from your lips!" I insist. "I want to hear how much you want me to be with one of them. Tell me I'm just a job for you."

She tries to wiggle her wrist away. "Let me go!"

I keep hold of her, my thoughts scattered. It's a fucking mess, but it's our mess, and I want her in the eye of the hurricane with me.

"Tell me, Callie. Who is your favorite?"

Her gaze goes from our joint hands to our wrists, then to my face. Her mouth closes in a thin line, and there's a storm behind her eyes.

"I fucking hated that you kissed her!" she roars at a volume significantly higher than our dared whispers.

I let her wrist go, and she advances on me. "You kissed me one day just to kiss her right after? Is that what you want to hear? How much I hated to watch that video over and over again? Does that make you happy?"

"It doesn't make me bloody happy, Callie!"

She pushes my chest with both her hands. "Do you want to hear how impossible it is to watch you dating all these women? To interview them about how goddamn dreamy you fucking are? What's the point? Why do you want to hear it from me?"

My chest is on fire beneath her palms, and I lose all reasoning. I forget why I wanted her to confess, and I forget why we shouldn't. I stalk toward her, and this time, she doesn't step back. In a flash, my hands are on her, bringing her up to face me. She meets me in the middle, my hands behind her thighs, and with a jump, her legs—her fucking legs—circle my waist.

She's breathless from fighting, and her eyes are hazy. Fast,

AMY OLIVEIRA

like someone who was raised in these rooms, I turn around, finding the pantry's entrance.

Callie gasps when the darkness engulfs us, and I rest her back on the single wall without shelves. I'm acting on pure memory of the place. It's pitch dark, and if Callie wasn't in my hands, I wouldn't be able to find her.

But she *is* here. Her ass in my palms, her hot breath on my neck. I hate the amount of clothes she has on. I've never hated a leather jacket this much. Once I have her pinned between me and the wall, I let one hand free, taking her beanie off to feel the soft strands of her hair between my fingers.

I trace her jaw in the dark. I feel her whimper even though I haven't done anything yet. She has a delicate neck, and my hand closes around it.

"You know what I really want, Calliope?" I say in her ear. My grip on her is not strong enough to hurt, but I can feel her pulse beating faster.

"W–what?" she whimpers out.

"I want you to stop spinning lies."

146

CHAPTER 14
Callie

Spinning lies.

He's between my legs, his hand placed possessively around my neck as I gulp at the dark tone of his voice. Nice, agreeable Sebastian is gone, and the man left behind is something else.

"I always tell the truth–" I start, but he's tsking before I even have a chance to finish the sentence.

"No," he growls. "You knew there was something between us. That's why you worked so hard to avoid me."

I swallow, grateful for the darkness. "I avoided you because we were crossing a line."

"What line?" he pushes. I'm paralyzed in his hands. His body is hot close to mine, he's hard as steel between my legs, and I'd be lying again if I said I wanted us to part.

"I've never gotten that close to an Eligible," I say lamely.

His chuckle is husky. "Probably because you never wanted to shag them."

"Sebastian..." I groan.

I'm at my wit's end. I'm angry at him for kissing Isla, angry

149

because I can't shout at him like I wanted. Angry because he's not mine. Except he is.

He's mine.

"I never want to kiss another person ever again, Callie," he promises, reading my mind.

"You will." I insist on trying to bring us both back to reality. "At least at the finale, you must."

"No one can make me kiss anyone."

"You signed a contract..."

"I signed a contract saying I'd finish the season, and I will. No one can make me fall in love with them. Not even you."

"Fuck, Sebastian, this is not good. My job, I–"

He silences me with a kiss. I hate how easy it is. He gets me to melt for him with just a kiss. Makes me forget my reason and the job I was hired to do.

I'm not a romantic person. I have told myself that for years. It's the perfect explanation of why I avoided relationships; I'm just career-focused. But then, Sebastian nips on my lower lip and calls my name with a growl, and I can't...I can't deny this anymore.

The showrunner is dating the casting director. Many members of the crew went out with eliminated girls before. How hard could it possibly be to believe that one day, someone would be interested in the Eligible?

Well, I barely believe it myself.

Not the Callie Sosa with a laser beam focus. Not the Callie Sosa with short words and a bright future.

I have a future in this network. How hard is it for a girl from the wrong side of town to get where I am now? I know how much I worked for this, and I beg myself to pump the breaks on us, but...

Don't I deserve happiness too? Don't I deserve to have it all?

I'm a scrambling mess when I put distance between Sebastian's lips and mine. He feels the change and lets me go, even though I'm still pressed between his chest and the wall, my legs still wrapped firmly around him.

His fingers leave my neck, and if I think I couldn't breathe before, now, it's even worse. I suck in a breath when he brings his hand up to my cheek, caressing with the back of his hand in such an intimate gesture, a lump forms in my throat.

"I know I'm being selfish, love," he whispers over my parted lips. "I looked at this at every possible angle, but..."

He doesn't say it out loud and neither do I. He knows it is wrong, just like I do. And still, we can't help ourselves. I stepped back from him for no good reason because I could feel in my bones we were going to cross a line.

Lie.

I wanted to cross the line. From the second I put my eyes on Sebastian, I knew he was the best-looking man I had ever seen, and I hoped he was a stuffy aristocrat with a king complex.

But no.

He's funny, easy to talk to, and so damn down to earth. We only needed to talk on the phone once, and I knew I never wanted to hang up.

I want to show him the city, the grossest burger joint I love. I want to bring him to my ridiculously small apartment, knowing full well he has never been in such a cramped space.

I want to introduce him to my brothers and not help in the slightest when Ben and Dario try to tear him a new one.

I want to be friends with his gorgeous sister and meet Maverick. And I desperately want them to like me.

I want to scandalize his parents with my accent, heritage, and bad attitude.

I really want to taint his bloodline.

I can say to myself it was Anya's warning until the cows

come home, but deep down, I know it was my fear that made me avoid him.

Sebastian Riggs is terrifying.

His breathing catches, and his forehead comes down to mine. I wish I could see his eyes. I need to see the struggle I feel in my bones reflected in that ocean blue.

But in the dark, I can only wish. His breath mingles with mine; one hand makes a mess of my hair.

"You need to be strong for both of us," he pleas. "I can't be the one who wrecks your life, but I don't think I can let you go."

And he'd destroy my life. I know, I know. My hands clutch his shoulders, and I feel deep inside that there's no way around it. We can't get out of this unscathed. I'm always going to be the producer who slept with the Eligible.

It will ruin my chances at *The Final Rose*.

It will taint my name with the network, with any other shows. My career will be ruined because all the stories involving crew members and the talent were always told by men to other men.

Being with Sebastian is writing a scarlet letter on my chest.

The answer is clear as day before me.

And yet, I kiss him.

My lips catch his, and I swallow his groan. Suddenly, my clothes are too restrictive, the leather jacket catching when my arms try to roam free. I beg over his lips, "Help me take this off."

Sebastian lets my legs go for a second, my feet meet the ground, and he has to bring his head down to keep kissing me. I'm off the wall. His hands are free to help me remove everything between us. The jacket, the stupid scarf, and a sweater I put underneath.

When the last layer is off my body, I hear his husky laugh. "It's not that cold, love."

I scoff, but I can't be bothered to talk about the weather right now. I'm on a mission to destroy my life, and I want to do it thoroughly.

My hands find his chest, so deliciously bare under my palms. His muscles bulge when I work my way down, feeling his skin, my senses tuned to what I can't see.

I reach for the elastic band, my thumbs making a line from side to side, and I hear his breath intake. My head whips up even in the dark, following the sound, and he comes close to me again, hand on the nape of my neck, fingers buried in my hair.

"Callie..." and I swear, he says it just to test it out. To remind himself it's me who's with him.

I whimper when he closes the space, his chest on mine covered only by a bra. He tugs my head up, holding me by the hair. My mouth falls open, and he takes the opportunity to take my lips once again.

I'm frantic after this. I want to sign my death certificate and fall into the night. I rise on my tiptoes to take more of him, my hands on his muscled back, his hands undoing my bra.

It falls between us, and I barely have a chance to fret about how I'm going to find my clothes in the dark. Sebastian breaks our kiss to go down to my neck as his left hand takes one breast.

He makes a sound that doesn't agree with his good boy image, and his mouth closes around my nipple while he tugs on the other. His hot mouth and the pad of his fingers trace infuriating circles, and the feeling travels down to my core.

"Sebastian..." I beg him between moans and whimpers.

His big hands go down my waist. He kneads my hips, and my body chases his.

"I got you, Callie," he whispers, and I hope he's telling the truth.

Those fingers go to the buttons of my jeans, and he undoes them in a flash. I'm hot all over, a pleading mess so high on him. His flesh, his taste, his warmth.

He tugs the jeans down my legs, and I'm relieved he's as desperate as me. Once my jeans are discarded alongside my shoes, I'm back in his arms, my legs back around his narrow waist as he presses me again to the wall like it's my place.

His teeth graze my jaw, his hand moving my face out of the way to fulfill his whims. And I let him, because at some point, a knot came undone.

Sebastian turns into a savage as he devours me. I love his rough side, the grunts, his tongue trying to trace all over my skin. If I'm expecting a gentleman, I'm mistaken.

I feel his hand coming between us, lowering his pajamas, and then I'm overcome by the feeling of him hot between us.

I hold my breath; he chuckles. Somewhere in my deep conscience, I know this is wrong. I can't be doing this. I shouldn't wish for things that aren't meant for me.

Even so, I let his hand between us tug my underwear to the side. I feel his finger making a path between my legs, and I throw my head back. Sebastian bites my jaw, and I move, practically hopping on top of him, begging like I never thought I would.

He doesn't give it to me straight away. His fingers tease my clit slowly, and I have to bite my lip down not to scream.

"I wish I could see you riding my hand," he says as the words break. His voice is low and raw.

"What? Oh God."

He pushes a finger inside me, long and deep, and I tremble in his hands. When he adds another one, I let a moan free. I imagine those corded arms working me, and my toes curl.

"I wish I could see you too."

As much as I love the darkness, I can only imagine what he

looks like. Sebastian is a god among men. He's perfect from every angle, every pose.

Something tells me he's not looking so perfect right now.

I feel his damp skin, my hands messing with his ever-so-flawless hair. I can hear the dryness in his tone, the want, in the pure animalistic way he says my name.

I wish I could see him losing control.

I grab his cock, tired of being tortured, afraid the moment will pass me by. His growl fuels my intentions, and I slowly pump him. He takes his fingers away, and I feel my own wetness when he carves into my thighs for leverage while angling his cock to my entrance.

He slips inside at an agonizing pace, his arms shaking, and I catch myself before I moan too loudly.

And then, I hear it.

Steps through the house, quiet wishes of good morning of the half-asleep crew.

I gasp, but he covers my mouth with his hand. I stay frozen, my eyes closing in fear as I hear my colleagues start their day, not far from the *doorless* pantry where I stand naked.

Sebastian's hand on my ass grips me to the point of pain. His mouth descends to the shell of my ear, and his voice is so low, I mostly feel the vibrations on my skin.

"Are you going to be quiet?"

I should say no.

I can't be quiet. I can't be still. I want to scream, moan, and move around. I want to fall apart in his arms.

But I nod my head quickly, his hand still over my mouth, knowing my promise means nothing.

And then, he buries himself to the hilt.

I'm glad he never moved his hand, because I'm a whimpering mess under his palm. My back arches, and I wish I could have seen his size before agreeing to remain quiet.

I feel his wet tongue making a path to my neck to bite my

earlobe. Sebastian moves slowly, punishing. "Shh, quiet. Don't say a word, Calliope." And when I nod again, he praises me, "That's my girl."

He sets a pace. I know I'm leaving marks on his back, but my nails are my only outlet.

Someone turns the kitchen lights on. They're coming in and making coffee. I hear their jokes, the rustling of clothes, and the clink of mugs.

Sebastian's hand leaves my mouth, and I almost ask him to bring it back. I can't trust myself.

I feel like a new woman, his thrusts turning me into someone I don't recognize. I bite my lip, my eyes locked onto the illuminated part of the almost empty pantry. The shelves are bare, but if anyone decides to come in, they could see us. They'd catch—

"Hey," Sebastian says, bumping his nose to mine.

And for the first time, I look his way.

We aren't in the darkness anymore. Even in the low light, I can see him perfectly now. His eyes are pinned on me, and my hands move from his shoulders to his face, taking it between my palms, feeling the roughness of his shaved jaw.

"Hi," I mouth.

And he drills into me while looking right at my eyes, the most intimate moment of my life. My hands go to his neck, his pulse thundering and his hips driving me into madness.

I feel his thickness from my head to my toes, his cock slamming into me and ripping me open, pussy and heart. The tears threaten to fall; I'm overwhelmed, lost in the feel and taste of him.

When my tongue comes out to wet my bottom lip, it's like he reads my mind. He kisses me, a hand coming to my chin, angling me to open up, but the tender moment doesn't interrupt how good he's fucking me. He kisses me like I'm precious and I'm about to break, and in a way, I am.

I feel my orgasm building. I feel it in my bones gathering and coming for me, and I have no way to stop it.

I can't hear the crew outside anymore. I don't notice the world turning around us.

Then, Sebastian's hands leave my chin, and he grabs the other side of my hips, bringing us a step away from the wall. My lower back is removed from it, the new angle merciless. My hands close in a fist, and he doesn't stop.

It's thrust after thrust. The tears finally drop when I unravel, and I have to clamp my hand over my mouth.

The orgasm is powerful, washing over me, baptizing our mistakes, cementing who we are now. He soon follows, head thrown back, mouth open in a silent scream, and it's beautiful to see.

I feel his release inside me, filling me up in a way I can't explain. His forehead comes to mine as he pumps through his orgasm, gently, slowly, and my breath comes out raggedly.

Someone drops a mug on the floor, the sound of ceramic breaking loud in the early morning.

I look at Sebastian in alarm, and he looks right back to me.

Then, everything else breaks too.

CHAPTER 15
Sebastian

I eliminate Mackenzie next.

The whole affair is very clinical. I know once upon a time, I complained about how mechanical it all felt, but I don't care anymore.

Anya says because of what happened to Isla, they will split the round of dates into two episodes. I will have a sweet elimination with Isla, where we both explain in separate interviews there was no chemistry, and then another episode will be with the rest of the girls, where I'll eliminate Mackenzie.

When I cross my arms and ask if Anya is trying to decide who I select, she tells me my date with Mackenzie was horrible, and I can't possibly justify keeping her after that.

I barely remember that date. I remember Mackenzie being horrible as usual, but mostly, I remember the absence of Callie. I remember looking everywhere to see a glimpse of her brown hair while Mackenzie went on and on about something or another.

Today isn't much different. We have a group date to fill the gap between eliminations, and it's excruciating. I play around in my head about eliminating someone else just to fuck with Anya, but I can't hear Mackenzie's voice anymore.

By the end of the night, she's gone, and it's one last thing to worry about. I barely remember the elimination.

Well, besides when she pushed me and told me I was going to regret it.

I kept a straight face and said, "Maybe." Because what else can one say to that? She didn't like my agreeable nature and trotted off in a tantrum.

Vera, Grace, Maya, and Abby remain. The host smiles and talks to the camera. The girls hug each other like it's some sort of celebration, and I feel my mouth dry.

I want out.

I desperately want out. My eyes scan the sitting room where we're having the elimination ceremony. Maverick's scenes were delayed another day, as Anya can't stop reminding me.

Callie is chatting with the assistant director, but I know she can feel the weight of my gaze. Her posture changes; her hands come to the back of her neck, like it's right there that I'm kissing.

I've been holding myself since she left the pantry when no one was watching and ran to the back door, just to stroll in after and say good morning to everyone like nothing had happened.

I wasn't that theatrical. I just went over and got myself a cup of tea, like strolling around with no shirt among the crew was something I did every day.

Sometime in the afternoon, Callie was able to take a shower, and thank God for that. I couldn't hold myself back when I knew she must smell like me.

It's a hunger, a desperation that threatens to take over, but in the back of my mind, I pray to be rational.

I need to take Callie and me out of this mess.

In a less dramatic sense than faking my death or other helpful suggestions from Maverick. When we are wrapping up and I know I have the rest of the night free, after such a long day, I make a beeline for Anya.

I don't know how to fix anything, but I know Anya is the key. She seems to run the show more than the showrunner himself, and her patience is thin.

Before I'm even in front of her, she calls, "Do you need anything, Mr. Riggs?" without looking at me.

"I certainly do." I feel she'll appreciate my directness.

Like I imagined, her head goes up, and she faces me, even if wary. I step closer, looking to my right and left, not missing Callie's alarmed face when she sees me talking to her boss.

"Who's next?"

"Excuse me?" She crosses her arm in front of her chest.

"Soon, I will have to eliminate another one. Only three girls go to the finale. I'm asking who."

"I don't know, Mr. Riggs. Why don't you ask your heart?"

I chuckle, because I can't stop myself. The woman can't be bullshitted, and while not dilly-dallying over a subject goes against my very English upbringing, I do it for Callie.

"Tell me your impressions. Your outsider view."

"Mr. Riggs, why would you think I would ever offer guidance of any type?"

"So, should I eliminate Vera?"

Her teeth grit. "If you're in love with someone else."

Yes, I am, but you won't like the answer.

Instead of antagonizing her even more, I breathe deeply, pinching the bridge of my nose as I lower my voice once more.

"I'm thinking Grace. I get along better with the other three."

"Very well." She dips her chin.

I know I need to leave it alone. I do not know what I accomplished during this conversation. I want Anya's trust. I

want to figure out if she'll crucify Callie or if she'll understand. But as it is, I've learned nothing.

"I thought you believed in love," she calls after I turn my
back.

"I do."

"I have horrendous stories about Sebastian if you ladies want
to hear!" Maverick booms like the king of the party.

"Don't you dare," I say, but with an affectionate chuckle.

The girls swarm him with questions. They want to know
about my childhood, my family, and everything in between.
Maverick tells them all the pre-approved stories about my
childhood, and I'm happy to take a step back.

In front of the cameras, my friend flourishes. All the girls
love him, and it's the first time I'm completely relaxed around
them.

A small marquee was raised in the garden, complete with a
barman and refreshing cocktails. And even though there's a
bitter wind, the skies are clear, and I almost believe it's a
summer garden party.

"You lot ready to move to England?" he asks.

While most of them nod agreeably, Vera tsks. "Well, it's a
serious conversation to have."

I nod. "Some people have very important jobs."

Vera swats my shoulder. "And it's cold here!" she says, and
the other girls agree and talk about their experiences since their
arrival.

Where to live is a great discussion I'll happily have with
Callie and Callie alone.

I let Maverick entertain the girls as I nurse one drink. By

ten at night, they are tired, and the shooting officially stops. We say our goodnights, and they all hug Maverick like old friends.

The cameras are down, and people are still moving about, but Maverick puts a beer in my hand before I say anything.

"They are lovely."

I nod, almost melancholically. "They are great."

He inhales and turns off his microphone, and I follow his lead. Looking around, he asks, "Where's your girl?"

"Shut it," I say without looking for Callie.

"Nah, they are all busy. Point her way."

My elbows are resting on my knees, the bottle dangling between my fingers. I let my gaze wander and find Callie in the crowd.

There she is.

Talking fast on the walkie-talkie, pointing in different directions, and answering many questions at the same time. The girl thrives every time she's on set. An invisible hand squeezes my heart.

"I can't fuck this up," I say so low, even Maverick has trouble catching my words.

After a second of looking at Callie, he turns away, his eyes wide open like he's seeing me for the first time.

"I wasn't dooming you."

I clear my throat instead of responding.

"I just wanted you to see how much of a big deal this is." He keeps talking. "Mate, if you say she's your girl, she's your girl. And we can think of ways to get her for you."

I stare at my friend and force a small nod. His hand lands with a powerful slap on my back. "Here's a lad. Now," and to the surprise of everyone, especially mine, he bellows, "Callie!"

I almost swallow my tongue, my alarm difficult to hide. I practically can hear the beating of Callie's heart as she comes to us. She tries to hide any emotion, but I can read her well.

"Sebastian here says it was you who delivered every flower bouquet I sent," he says loud enough to be overheard.

"Well, apparently, it was my job to be Riggs' delivery girl," she replies with all that sassiness that makes me crazy.

My mouth curves, and Maverick nods. "Well, you better sit down and tell me about his reactions in detail."

Maverick points to the chair at the front, and that's when Callie falters. She looks on both sides, but someone from the crew comes to the rescue.

"You have a beer, Sosa," he says. "Save one for me."

She nods, relieved. Sitting down and grabbing a drink, my girl smiles coyly. "He cried each time."

"You don't say? Sebastian has always been the sensitive one."

Callie nods effusively. "It's rare to see a man in tears with no provocation."

"It's freeing to hear."

"Oh, sobbing over the roses." Callie continues. "Once, he held the flowers, and sang to—"

"Ok, ok..." I interrupt them. "That's enough from you both."

"I spend my hard-earned money lavishing you with lovely pressies, and that's what you have to say?"

"Thank you for the flowers, Maverick. I'm actually upset you haven't sent any since I've been back."

"He only takes," Maverick turns to Callie. "Never gives."

"Oh, I'm giving," I say with a smirk.

"Well, I won't get into that," Maverick murmurs.

Surprising me, instead of feeling uncomfortable, Callie laughs away, clinking her bottle to Maverick's.

"I'm going to like you, Maverick."

I meet Devi, Dora, and a bunch more people who ended up getting one last drink before tucking in. My heart feels light. I'm happy I can just hang out with Callie without lurking in the shadows. It feels like before, when our banter was easy. Before I decided she was mine.

Maverick fits into any crowd. His arms open on the back of the comfortable couch, the set crew giving up on tidying up the place and sitting down for a drink too. And for a moment, I dare to wish this was it. That I was a regular bloke in love with a girl and having drinks with her friends.

I can't say *The Final Rose* is the worst decision I ever made. It was probably the best. But sometimes, it's hard to look at the logo without wincing.

"Maybe you should hire me as your manager." Maverick taps my knee. "Just to sort through the fan letters."

"Excuse me?"

"The teaser came out today," Devi explains, and before I have a chance to ask, someone shoves a device in my face. It's already playing when I turn to have a proper look.

It starts like any other season's teaser, with the voiceover from the host: "The fairy tale begins..."

Shots of the best angles of the mansion flash. Then, the first group of girls. Mackenzie says, "I hope he's handsome."

And then, someone gasps. Another girl I can't identify says, "Oh my God!" in a staged whisper.

The screen changes to the interviews set back in the mansion. Vera is smiling at the camera as she says, "I just want to fall in love."

My stomach plummets, but I don't have time to react, as

the teaser is still going, talking about the twelve girls, showing shots of them looking nothing but magnificent.

Finally, it's my feet coming down the main stairs. The camera pans from my shoes until it finally reaches my torso. I'm fixing my cufflinks like a proper knob with the grossest smile on my lips: "Hello, ladies."

Sparkles, *The Final Rose*.

I keep the device in my hands for longer than necessary. It's not exactly bad. No. It's quite on-brand, actually.

Yet, I have to hold myself back from cringing.

For the first time, I wonder what the girls are saying amongst themselves. They are on camera all the time, from morning until night. They sleep together and share all kinds of conversations, while I only interact with them on scheduled dates.

They share an intimacy I don't have with any of them. It's clear they got closer as the months went by, and it comes to me now that they might have a different view of this show.

People comment on the teaser, they shake hands, happy about how good it all looks, and make a toast to the best season yet.

Like he senses my mood going down, Maverick faces me with a serious expression. "Listen, I wasn't happy about that sleazy smile either."

I can't help but chuckle, and then I drink a little more and hope to forget.

It's way past anyone's bedtime when we are done. I wouldn't think it would be ok for us to stay so late drinking, but the only thing they complained about was the possibility of an early morning.

I watch them filing out, and Maverick stays back with me. I feel bad for the girls too. They went to bed too early, and it almost felt like we were keeping them away.

Callie is holding onto Dora. They are laughing and talking, barely noticing the world around them. Another crew member comes around and takes Dora into his arms, claiming she's a lousy drunk, but it's all in good nature.

The floor clears out soon, and Callie looks back at me and Maverick, still there.

Her cheeks are rosy from the cold or alcohol, and her hair is unkempt under the beanie. I can't explain how perfect this woman is.

She's small and sweet, voracious and strong. She's so many things, I can barely keep up.

She slices me open with a look. She can tear my chest apart in a second. No one ever has had that much power over me.

Maverick slaps my back. "Go on, then." He's not even finished, and I'm already walking.

I see he's following, but my eyes are on Callie. She's hanging beside the back door, her eyes sparkling from the garden lights. I stop in front of her, and I say nothing.

"Goodnight, Cals." Maverick comes behind me. Callie smiles up at him and mouths goodnight.

Maverick goes up the stairs as Callie's mouth turns down into a line.

"We can't stay here alone," she says, but like me, she doesn't move.

"We were all drinking late. Everyone was together. Here..." I tug her arm, pulling her inside the house and closing the back door after me.

There's no point standing in the cold.

The lights are out in the spacious sitting room, our faces illuminated only by the lights outside. It feels like a bad omen that we can only be together in the darkness.

"I need to go to bed," Callie whispers. "I share a room with the other--"

I kiss her. She's right; she's always right. But I watched her for a full day and night, wanting nothing more than to kiss and hold her, and I can't take it anymore.

Callie melts in my arms, setting herself free for just a second. We kiss, and it's perfect. The blood rushes through my veins, and I want more.

I need to fuck her again. As animalistic as it sounds, the need is strong. I'm tired of sneaking out and pretending I'm not in love with Callie Sosa.

She ends the kiss, massaging her temple as she shakes her head. "This is insane."

I rub her arms, wishing I could banish the bad thoughts from her head. "I know it's not ideal..."

"Not ideal doesn't begin to cover it, Sebastian!"

"I'm working on a way."

"There's no way. Not without me losing my job."

My hands go to her face, and I angle it up. "I won't let this hurt you. You won't lose your job."

"I lose something either way," she says in the most heart-breaking way, her eyes going moist before she shakes from my hold and hides her emotions.

"Callie, can you please believe me? I'm telling you, I'll find a way. You won't lose your job. And you won't lose me."

It's important that she understands it. I can't fix things around us when I think she's a flight risk.

"I want to believe it," she confesses. "I want nothing but to believe everything is going to work out. But Sebastian, this is bad. As bad and career damaging as it could be."

"I will find a way. We aren't doing anything wrong!"

She scoffs and steps away. I feel the cold in my bones. I'm losing her.

"Callie..."

"It's on me," she says firmly. "I'm the one who needs to decide what I can live without."

This is my chance to be altruistic. To tell her I'll leave her alone, and she can go live her life and never hear from me again.

But I don't want to leave her alone. I take her hands again, tugging her into my arms, and she can't help but to come.

"Just give me time. And faith. That's all I'm asking."

Her lips part, and I'm holding my breath for an answer. Something out there makes a noise, probably something falling. Callie jumps away from me, but I hold her still. My hand is on her chin, and I can't let her go without an answer.

"Time and faith, Callie. That's all I'm asking."

And she finally nods. First, it's like she only wants me to let her go, but her eyes chase mine. They are filled with emotion, and I know she's putting all her faith in me.

I release a calming breath, my arms around her going soft as she steps away.

I trace her features with my eyes. The high cheekbones, the small curve of her chin. Deep brown eyes and the cutest little nose. She gives me only a second more, watching from under her eyelashes, and then, she's gone.

Disappeared. Up the stairs and out of sight.

I rake my hand over my head and give her a minute head start. Eventually, I go to my bedroom, climbing the stairs like it's a sacrifice.

My mind is in turmoil when I close the bedroom door behind me. I asked for time and faith, but it can't be that much time. We can't be like this much longer.

I'm still fully dressed when I hear the knock on my door.

A fire lights up, and I pray to all the gods it's Callie. She's giving me a night. A couple of hours in bed.

I open the door to the dark hallway, but it isn't Callie looking back at me in an emerald green housecoat. It's not the soft brown eyes I'm used to and not the messy hair.

It's Vera.

"I know you're having an affair with Callie Sosa."

CHAPTER 16
Callie

After a week in Sebastian's country house, Grace is eliminated in a long ceremony that no doubt will translate into a double episode to announce the top three.

Vera, Abby, and Maya.

The girls hug each other and Sebastian. The crew applauds what was our last night in England. Tomorrow, the three girls and Sebastian are scheduled for a photoshoot in the gardens, and then we are all heading to the airport, back to Los Angeles.

I breathe in and out, reminding myself it's all under control. Sebastian asked me to trust him, and I want to honor that promise. But I also want to bolt.

Run far away. Run from my work, from Sebastian and all these cameras.

I remain still, though. I show little to no emotion as we finish up shooting. I feign a headache to avoid another night of drinking with the crew. This time around, people are going to a bar in the village, but the idea turns my stomach.

I stay behind, and I toss and turn for hours and hours in

my bed. For a delirious minute, I contemplate going after Sebastian to share my worries with him. When I decide it might be too risky, I get anxious, thinking he might be the one coming to me.

He never comes.

I barely have an hour of sleep, and then it's time for the damned photoshoot.

I hate everything in the morning. The coffee tastes like tea, just like everything else in England. The mornings are impossibly cold, and the heaters make a weird noise when they heat completely, and it always startles me.

I bury my nose in the scarf around my neck and pull my beanie down. I won't be convinced this is not the worst of winter. But then, I look and see some people are actually walking with just long-sleeved shirts, even a couple in regular t-shirts.

That annoys me as well.

I'm aware my awful mood isn't anyone's fault, so I keep out of everyone's way, offering to do jobs that require the least interaction.

I organize our transport to the airport and call the cleaning crew, confirming their arrival later this afternoon.

I direct the assistants. I check the packed equipment and assemble a crew to film the photoshoot in case we need extra footage.

But during my third gross cup of coffee, as I yell to the assistants not to make a mess out of the luggage, I hear a throat clearing behind me, and I know it's time to face the music.

I expect to see Anya telling me off, reminding me this isn't my job, demanding an explanation. But it isn't Anya.

It's Nessa.

She tilts her head, watching me with an expression I am not sure what to think of. She works in the industry too, so she's literally my only friend left that won't be upset when I miss another baby shower, or rehearsal dinner or wedding.

It's hard to keep friends with this job, and Nessa gets it. We are the lowest maintenance friends, and that is already too much.

"Can we talk?" she asks, and I can't stop myself from shifting on my feet.

I don't want to talk. I usually jump at any chance to hang out with her, but I'm scared of what she'll *see*.

I need work to occupy my mind away from the fact that the person who was inside me not that long ago is taking romantic pictures with other women.

But when I open my mouth to refuse, I end up closing back up and just nodding, leading the way from the luggage and my other random tasks.

We put distance between the photo shoot and me. With each step, my heart feels lighter, and my head clearer.

"What's happening, Callie?" she asks after five full minutes of silence.

I contemplate lying. Denying. Laughing it off. But the crisp, icy wind I was cursing just a minute ago now is actually clearing my head. The distance we put ourselves from the crew makes me braver.

And I turn to my friend and tell the truth. "I think I fucked up."

Nessa doesn't say a word as I tell her. Now that it's open, I can't stop myself from confessing it all. I tell her how Anya told me to get closer to him and how close I got so quickly.

I try to explain how easy it is with him, but I can't put it into words. Something connected us from the second we met. It wasn't on purpose. I need her to get that part.

For years, I got close to the contestants, kept control over the narrative, and remained professional. I knew better than to get attached. But when Anya called me to get my head in the game, I took it as a blow to my heart.

When I finish my mangled tale, Nessa doesn't say a word for a beat. All I hear are our steps on the grass and a distant bird song. I take a minute to breathe in and out, tilting my head up to the gray skies and chanting a prayer.

"Are you going to do it?" she asks, finally breaking the silence.

I open my eyes and turn to her. "Do what?"

"Trust him to fix it."

I stop in my tracks with a frown. "That's all you're going to say? I'm literally sleeping with the talent. This can ruin my career."

"Oh, God!" Nessa rubs her face, looking frustrated. "They want us to stay at work all the time, and then it's a surprise when we fuck at work too?"

I can't stop myself from widening my eyes. The harsh words aren't her style.

"I'm tired of trying so hard to be a robot." Her shoulders sag. "I gave my whole life to this place. I work hard just to have the privilege of hearing from my family how upset they are because I'm old and childless." She rolls her eyes. "At some point, I get lonely. We all do, so—"

She doesn't say more, because I can fill in the blanks. She gave herself to this job. It's hard to keep friends. We have very little free time and a lot of travel to do. We alienate everyone in our lives. Then, one day, you dare to connect with someone.

"I knew people were going to assume I was sleeping with Adam for the wrong reasons," she admits. That's the first time she has admitted to being with the showrunner. "But we work so well together. It was so good, and I didn't want the network to take anything else from me. I love my job, and I know you love it too, Callie. But there needs to be a line. We are women working in an unforgivable industry, but sometimes, the call comes from inside the house, you know?"

I consider her words. "Do you think I am judging myself?"

She shrugs. "I know *I* judged myself a lot. I kept looking at Adam as the showrunner and not a single man I liked a lot. A man who made me feel good and had a lot in common with me. I felt so ashamed, like I was truly sleeping my way to the top, but when I thought about it, if it wasn't among the crew, when the hell would I have time to date?"

I nod and resume our walk. "You're right. I get what you're saying, but this is different. Sebastian isn't one of the crew. He's the reason for the show. He's the Eligible. He's here to fall in love, and it's not with me."

Nessa rolls her eyes. "Again, we aren't robots. Shit happens."

"He has a contract." I brace myself. "He needs to choose between three names. Abby, Vera, or Maya."

"His contract says he needs to choose a name for the finale. No one can enforce a relationship afterward."

I stop again. "You know better than me. It's the show's name rolling in the mud. He can't turn a week after the finale and go out with a producer. I'm going to lose my job."

"It's not your fault you fell in love!" She puts her foot down like a badly behaved child.

I face my sneakers, green from all the damp grass. Before, I wasn't brave enough to give a name for what I felt about Sebastian, not when it feels like I'm out of control. Every day is a rollercoaster, fast, gripping me by the throat.

So yeah, maybe I am in love with Sebastian Riggs. But I refuse to say the words while our destiny is uncertain and I'm about to lose him at any second.

"No," I say as he sits down.

"No?"

"You need to turn around and go."

Sebastian watches me from above. He waits in the middle of the corridor as the flight attendants are helping the other passengers store their luggage.

"I thought you wanted to spend time with me."

"I don't," I lie.

He sits beside me anyway. I let a breath go and can't resist looking right and left to see where the rest of the crew is.

And they are all around us.

Last time, Anya and the other members went a week ahead to get a few locations organized before the shooting.

Our team was diluted, the big names in first class and the rest of us scattered through economy.

This time around, we are all together. Every cameraman, every assistant. My boss and her boss and everyone who is part of *The Final Rose.*

A P.A. named Tania is chatting with Tulio, a cameraman, just in the seat in front of us. Devi is with Doris in the seats across. There's not a place where I don't see a familiar face.

"Sebastian, they will—"

"Calm down, Callie," he says with a chuckle. "I'm not staying. I'd figured this time around was too busy to try anything funny. But I asked for an hour to talk to you. I just said it was about the show, ok?"

I nod fast, and my forehead falls to the seat in front of me as I take a deep breath.

"I'm sorry you're so stressed, love."

He called me that before, but I didn't give any notice.

Now, after my talk with Nessa, the word seems to weigh more. I straighten my back and scan the plane again, seeing if anyone is paying attention to us.

When I'm sure they are ignoring everything around them, I relax a little. "I'm ok."

It's a lie; I'm a mess.

"Good." He nods.

I face my left, really taking him in for the first time. He looks exhausted.

"Is everything ok?"

It takes Sebastian a second to reply. "It will be ok soon. We just need to hold on."

I bite my lip and nod again. I know this is a disaster. Sometimes, I think there's no way to get out of this mess unscathed.

Sebastian's voice goes down a notch. "You know I'm going to take care of you, right?" he vows. "I won't let anything happen. I won't destroy your career."

I know his intentions are pure. I know he would never hurt me intentionally.

Before I have time to formulate a reply, he captures my chin between his fingers. The feeling of his warm hand on my skin calms me quickly. I close my eyes and let the sensations take over.

"I know you're anxious, and you have every right to be. It doesn't escape me that you have more to lose than I do. I appreciate the trust you put in me, love. I know you could just turn around and not give me the time of day. I'm well aware."

The breath hitches, and I'm shaking my head, opening my eyes to his. "I can't. I really can't. I don't know what's wrong with me, but I can't. I'm here and..."

And I want to stay with you.

Those are the words I don't say. I told myself my whole life I'd never put my goals at risk. My future, the future of my family. And yet, my eyes fill with tears as I shake all over.

177

His thumb caresses my bottom lip, my tongue peeking out unbidden because I miss his taste. I see his dark pupils dilating so obviously in the sea of blue. A second goes by, and we just look at each other. I hold my breath, hold myself still, marking our moment in time.

I really want to stand up and say I don't care, announce that we're together and that's that. But I don't. I wait.

Sebastian smiles, and then his hand lowers. We both clear our throats and look away. My heart is thumping in my chest and my hands shake. I control my voice and, louder than before, I turn to him and start talking about our upcoming schedule.

We have an hour together, and even though we can't be ourselves, it doesn't matter.

He goes back to his seat eventually, and I miss him the second he's gone.

Ten hours later, I'm angry. I'm hungry. I'm full of nervous energy, but the good type.

I grab my luggage from the belt, and I know what I am going to do.

I'm going to have sex tonight.

I'm going to invite Sebastian Riggs to my tiny apartment and fuck his brains out.

CHAPTER 17

Sebastian

I eye her building, already knowing she'll need to move. Callie won't appreciate it, but this place simply won't do.

She wasn't lying before. It's in the worst neighborhood, with drug dealers doing business at her doorstep. My car won't make it through the night in a place like this. I can't believe a five-foot-nothing woman can.

The state of the building reflects the rest of the street. Decay and mess. The halls are dirty, and there's no intercom. People just come and go as they please.

I go up to the second floor, ready to lecture her as I ring the doorbell.

She can come to the hotel with me, and we can think of something else later. Maybe we can get a place together. It doesn't need to be full of luxury. I just want her to be safe, and I can't...

My thoughts are cut short when Callie opens the door and flings herself at me. Her arms band around my neck, her legs around my waist. She's quick. One second, I'm planning to pack her bags, the next, I don't want to ever leave the apartment.

When her lips are on mine, I groan, my hands firmly under her ass as I move inside and kick the door close. Callie giggles, taking my earlobe between her teeth.

"I still need to lock it. It doesn't matter how hot your move was," she tells me, wiggling away from my arms to grab the keys she keeps on a hook beside the front door.

"Believe me, I know you need to lock it up."

I can't stop myself. She's locking the door, and I grab her hips, bringing them to me. She bucks, turning the key as I rub her against me.

"So, you love my place?" Her voice hitches.

"Love it. You have to move."

I'm dead serious, but Callie laughs. With another pull, I rub her ass slowly over my cock, and her chuckle disappears into a moan. She tries to swirl around to face me, but I take her hands in mine and place them on the door in front of her face. I secure both her wrists, and her breathing catches.

"You live in a shithole, love," I let her know.

"Some of us don't get huge Georgian houses for our eighteenth birthday."

"If you only knew someone who has one of those English houses." I squeeze her wrist for a second. "Keep those here." My instructions leave no room for argument as I move my hands down to her shoulders.

She's wearing the smallest thermal top and those indecent denim shorts of hers. Bare feet, her toenails painted light blue.

"You think I suck dick for money, Riggs?"

I bite her shoulder. "Not for money. Maybe for a roof."

Her laugh is cracked, especially when I let my hands wander a little south. I grab her ass, her shapely legs, and then move back up to her waist. I decide I've had too much of that top, and I remove it. Callie unglues her hands from the door for just a second, but as soon as her top is off, she's back in position.

"You're such a good girl for me, Calliope," I tell her low in her ear.

Callie shakes beneath my palms, whimpering with praise.

"Can I turn?" she asks.

I move both my hands to her front, taking her tits in my palms, tugging her nipples as a simple word leaves my lips. "No."

Her throat works, but she doesn't move a muscle. I feel something coming over me. After months of not being in control of anything, I finally am.

I trace her neck with my nose, breathing her in as I bring one hand down her stomach to the button and zipper of her shorts. I tug them down along with her underwear, and I need a minute to process what's in front of me.

She's bent around the waist, her hands against the door and legs parted. I swallow a lump as I take in the small of her waist, the dimples in the base of her back, the perky ass and rounded hips. Callie is all perfection. Her body, her mind, her sense of humor. I need to hold myself back, try not to pounce and devour her whole.

"Sebastian?" she calls for me.

"I'm here," I reply, not taking my eyes off her.

"You're freaking me out."

I can't help it. I chuckle. I get closer again, my hands gliding over her hot skin.

To see Callie Sosa every day when she's forbidden? No man was ever so tortured. I refuse to think about that when she's so deliciously naked in front of me. She's so good at holding herself to the door like I told her.

I go down to my knees, her perfect ass just in front of my face. I take the leap and kiss her there, soft, almost a whisper, and Callie moans.

I do it again, so slowly, so softly that I know I'm making her crazy. It's making me crazy too, but I want to keep playing.

I close my hands over her hips, bringing them back to me. I look up and see her hands still on the door as she supports her body like that.

"Open up for me, love."

She sucks in a breath and obeys, pulling her legs further apart. Callie is mine. That's all there is to it. Nothing is getting in my way. They asked me to choose, and I did. I choose *her* every single day if I have to.

Callie moves her knees apart, but even then, I keep my hand in place over her ass. I draw circles over her skin, down her legs, inside her thighs. She moans and melts every time my thumb grazes her pussy.

"You're happy torturing me?" she asks breathlessly.

"It's not easy for me," I confess.

"I don't believe you," she says over her shoulder, a small smile playing on her lips.

"Hold on there, Calliope," I instruct. "Don't you dare move your hands. Can you do that?"

She bobs her head up and down, eager.

I grip her hips. She has to open her legs even more to make space for me. She says my name, but I don't give her much time.

I taste her pussy like I always wanted to, and she bucks trying to get out of my reach, but I keep her in place.

She tastes delicious, just as sweet as I thought she would. Her moans give me pleasure I didn't know was possible as I part her cheeks, gripping her ass.

I palm myself over my jeans, hard as a rock. I work her quicker, and she slaps the door. Her moans are so loud, I know the walls are too thin to contain them.

I want them all to know Callie is mine.

I take my cock out, stroking as I eat her out.

"Sebastian... Oh God." her voice is different now, softer outside the set.

"You taste so good. I'm pumping my cock. I couldn't wait."

"Are you?" She moves, trying to have a look, but I hold her in place. I'm not done with her, and I'll never be done with us.

I circle her clit with the tip of my tongue at the same time I pump myself faster.

And then, I hear it, low and perfect, my name trapped in her mouth, and I'm renewed. She's loud when she comes, sweetness right on my tongue.

I think of the ways I'm going to take her tonight. My mind promises forever, but my body can't think of anything beyond the next five minutes.

I'm holding on by a thread, but she's riding out her orgasm, and I need to hold her. I rise to my height to offer support, taking her body to mine. With a satisfied sigh, Callie slumps over my chest, her knees soft, and I chuckle.

I kiss her sweaty temple, my arm going around her waist. She looks edible like this, and I taste her shoulder, nipping it enough to earn a yelp from her. Then, I curl my arm under her knees, lifting her.

"Now, please, madam, direct me to your quarters."

She has a three-room apartment. The sitting room and kitchen together, an open door to a bathroom, and another mysterious door to the left. I don't need to be a genius to know door number two is the place to go.

"Oh, kind sir," she starts, even with her nose buried in my neck. "Can you kindly take me to the west wing?"

I scoff. "Your English accent is rubbish."

She swats my chest. "Hey, mate, let's get this hm—let's get cracking...mate."

I'm laughing when we enter her room, and I throw her on the bed. Even though I hate her building, I really like her little apartment. It's small but perfect for her. I can see her personality in every corner, every piece of furniture.

"You're still dressed," she says.

"Outrageous," I mock, joining her.

I lay on my side, supported by my elbow as she looks up at me with glassy eyes.

"It is."

I kiss her because she's beautiful and because I can. Her fingers find my shirt, and she undoes one button at a time. Her lips are still locked on mine, her legs circling me, changing positions. My back hits the mattress as she straddles me.

When the last button is released, Callie's hands travel over my chest as my hands find her legs, feeling her soft skin under my palms.

She's breathtakingly gorgeous. Her brown hair falls over her face, her body over mine. That smile. That goddamn perfect smile and all that wit.

I hold her in place, taking a nipple between my lips. She cries out, and I take the other.

"Ride me, Callie," I tell her.

And she's quick to follow that instruction too.

My fly is down, and it's not difficult for her to take my cock into her small hands. I hiss when I feel her holding me, thinking nothing can be as good as this.

Then, she sinks down on my cock, my groan and her moan mixing. Her blunt nails scratch my chest, her hips working us toward release. Her tits bounce in front of me, and I take one in my mouth again, her hand buries into my hair.

She tastes like mine. She moans my name so prettily. Her pussy is perfect around my cock.

I thought I lost myself in Callie, but I understand now.

I finally found myself.

It is still dark outside, and I wake up with my cock hard. Callie rubs her ass against me in her sleep, not realizing what she's doing.

My fingers carve into her hips, bringing her even closer. My cock slips between her thighs, her legs squeezing me hard, making my eyes roll to the back of my skull.

She's vulnerable like this. I roll her nipple between my fingers, and I swear, she gasps.

I can't take it anymore.

I bring two fingers to her clit, circling it slowly before I dip between her folds. I groan when I realize how wet she is. This woman is my dream come true. She's perfect in every way, and I can't deny it.

My nose is buried in her neck, and I ride the high only her skin against mine can provide. It's not enough, though; it's not even close.

"Callie, love," I murmur.

She replies with a moan, and I go back working on her clit. Her leg twitches, I chuckle, and she's finally waking up.

I lick her skin, savoring the damp saltiness for a moment, and then I'm on my knees, turning her around as her legs fall open. She breathes out in a dreamy way, and I hold her knees up as a second later, I'm inside her where I belong.

Her eyes are half open, and she grips the sheets as I bury myself to the hilt.

"I'm sorry. I couldn't wait anymore. I need to be inside you."

"Oh God..." She moans so sweetly, I'm renewed from the inside out.

Light comes slowly through the gaps of her window, golden sunlight streaking her skin.

When I come, she comes with me. Emotions roll into me, something different and stronger than I ever experienced. We belong together. I know it in my bones, my skin, my heart.

She cuddles into me, a relaxed smile on her lips, and fuck, I know I can't ever let her go.

CHAPTER 18
Sebastian

I'm sent back to my hotel by the end of our week off. I never wanted to do anything less than drag my arse back to the sterile halls of a hotel, but Callie says it's for the best.

During the week, she tried to withdraw into herself several times, but I was determined not to let it happen. I can't have her pretending this never happened.

We are happening. We are *now,* and not even her fear—as justified as it is—can stop this. I distract her with all the inventive ways I have in my arsenal and all the things I wanted to do since I laid my eyes on her. But eventually, the days go by, and the shadow above us only grows.

We are going back to the mansion.

I need to finish this game I signed up for. I need to choose between three women, and none of them is Callie.

Our kiss before I leave her apartment is desperate. She clings to me, taking my shirt in her hands, biting my lip like she needs to brand me to make me hers.

I raise her chin with my finger. "This is not the end. This is our beginning."

She nods then shakes her head, like she's shaking the feelings off. "I'm being silly, I guess."

Callie escapes my finger, her eyes downcast as she does her best to ignore the voices in her head.

"I'll always come for you, Callie." I try to make her understand. "Nothing in the world can't stop me from being with you, you get that?"

I know those are big words, and they might even feel displaced in the hall of America's worst apartment building. I mean them, though.

She looks at me from under her eyelashes, her eyes shining, and I know she wants to believe me. I don't know if she can. I insist anyway.

"Love, listen to my words carefully. I wanted to find you, and I did. And it might look like a mess right now, but there's nothing in the world that can stop this from happening. The only person who can take me from you is you. Are you going to ask me to fuck off?"

I smirk, and she snorts, shaking her head. I hate how vulnerable she looks at this moment. Callie is all strength, but right there, she looks like a scared little girl. I miss my sassy woman.

"Nothing. Get me? No one."

"We finish this season, and then we'll–"

"We'll be together. No contracts."

Her small smile is watery, but I get a gentle kiss on my lips before I leave.

The next day, I slide into the town car from my hotel to the mansion. Again, we are starting at an ungodly hour. The sun hasn't risen yet, and the streets are surprisingly empty. I don't think about anything but Callie.

Finish this damn show. Abby, Maya, or Vera.

Long were the days the network insisted on releasing it slowly, an episode a week. Eleven years ago, *The Final Rose* was a weekly ordeal like any show, but today, it's all about binging. The thirteen episodes will be released in three blocks and then the reunion separately.

It's probably stressful for everyone involved, but to me, it's fantastic. It means I won't need to wait months and months holding the finale's secret. The contract only stated I needed to hold my social media for the first week after release.

Soon, I'll be free.

Just one more week of dates. One finale. We just need to hold as the show is edited, and then it's done.

When I arrive at the mansion, I open the door to come face-to-face with one of the assistants. He has a clipboard and a closed expression. Something tells me even though it's still dark outside, this man was up hours ago.

"Anya is calling for you," he delivers robotically.

I fix my cufflinks so I have a way to deal with my nervousness. I want to be done with this already. Talking to Callie's boss is the last thing I need.

I give the assistant a stiff nod, and he turns on his heels. I understand I am to follow.

The first floor is exactly the way I remember: lights, cameras, and so many people. They bring flowers and fix things I would never know needed fixing. Something I learned after all this time with a filming crew is that chaos is never chaos. They have a way to move, a procedure to their madness. It's magical to see. The mansion now is bubbling with life, but it will turn into a dream when the cameras are on.

We climb the stairs to the most remote part of the mansion, away from where the girls sleep and other parts that are used to film. I've never been here. It's only used by the crew.

The assistant knocks at the door, and I hear Anya barking acceptance from the other side. He swings the door open but makes no move to enter with me. It's a bad sign how reluctant he is. I look at him for just a second, but his eyes are cast down.

He's throwing me with the lions.

A very pissed off lioness.

I can tell she's angry from the moment my eyes land on Anya. Her mouth is closed in a line. She looks at me so furiously, I almost miss that in front of her is…Callie.

My blood turns to ice at the same time as the door clicks closed behind me. I try to remember everything that it is to be a Riggs.

Never show weakness.

Never look rattled.

Always be pleasant.

Never kneel.

I dip my chin toward the woman. "You asked for me?"

She doesn't reply. Her eyes dissect me, pin me in place. With a tired sigh, I adjust my cuffs again, trying my best to look unconcerned.

"Any problems with the schedule?"

Anya snorts, so sarcastically that my eyes jump to Callie, who I was trying to ignore until now. But she's not looking at me. She's looking ahead, her eyes huge pools of warm brown.

"I'm not someone to keep the mystery, I guess." With that, she puts a tablet on the table directly in front of Callie.

It's my voice I hear first.

"I'm sorry you're so stressed, love."

All my blood leaves my body. My fingers flex, and the image comes into focus. I can barely make out our features, but it's us. The video was taken from behind. At times, part of my nose or Callie's cheeks are visible from the gap between the seats.

But our voices are clear, and while we say nothing specific, it's clear something is going on. I can hear my desperation, my love in every word I say to her.

Finally, I put the last nail in my coffin.

In our coffins.

"You know I'm going to take care of you, right? I won't let anything happen. I won't destroy your career."

I don't know if the video keeps going, but Anya decides it's enough.

"He *will* destroy your career." It's the first thing she says, her eyes glued to Callie.

My girl's gaze is still on the tablet. I see her working a lump in her throat, and my heart shreds to bits with her suffering.

"Who showed you this?" I finally ask.

"Does it matter?"

No, not really, but I don't have any other words.

"This ends now." She starts again. "Whoever sent it isn't a concern."

"You can't make decisions about our lives." I'm saying before I can stop myself. "We won't be together until the end of –"

She interrupts, her eyes filled with ice when they look at me. "Callie is talented. She's a hard worker, and she has a future. This," she pokes at the tablet, "will destroy her reputation. She will always be the producer who slept with the Eligible. Who will hire the producer who destroyed her own show?"

Callie hiccups, and I find myself going to her. Going to my knees, I try to find her eyes, but they are still frozen looking at the tablet. It's like we're not even here. If it wasn't for the hiccup, I'd assume she wasn't listening.

"Callie, I won't let this happen. I won't, I promised you."

"You can't protect her. Not in this. Not in this damn industry."

"I can bloody try!" I roar to the producer when Callie shows no reaction.

"I have worked in this town for the last thirty years. I've seen women blacklisted for less."

I scowl, rising to my feet. "I will fulfill the contract. I will finish the season and wait until it's aired. *The Final Rose* can't have a hold on me forever."

"No. It has a hold on *her*. You can walk free." She waves her hand like it's my fault, like I would put Callie in this situation.

"You'll stain her name."

"I will protect Callie–"

I don't have a chance to finish. "Walk away. This is her job. This is her life. There's no way to come out of this without repercussions. Not for her. Unless you secretly own a network and are ready to employ her."

I swallow dry and look down at Callie. I would never have thought I could talk around her like this. Never thought I would see the day she would let two people talk about her like she's not in the room.

She let us, though. Let us talk and talk and argue about her future.

I want to shake her. I want to ask her to react. I'm begging for her cleverness, but she gives me nothing. I'm falling because I feel like I lost her already.

She was so scared and put her faith in me, but I never came up with anything. I keep promising her career won't end, but I never explain how I am going to prevent that.

Anya is right. I don't own a network. I can't grease the hands of everyone in Hollywood to look the other way. My name is everywhere *The Final Rose* is concerned, my face in every teaser. I am the Eligible who is supposed to fall in love with one of the contestants and, while sure, they can't force me to fall in love, dating a producer is a completely different ball game.

"We can wait." I don't like the begging quality of my voice.

"It won't be weird if we get together in a year. It won't end her career."

Anya shrugs. "You're right. It might be ok. But for now, you need to back off."

"That's not of your business--"

"Anya is right."

It comes like a dagger firmly stabbed in my heart. It breaks skin; it goes deep into my flesh. Callie's voice is raw, so low that we could almost miss it, but it's there. And she's killing me.

"Someone was watching us. Someone noticed something and recorded us..." She licks her lips and swallows. "If someone here did this, I don't see how we could hide."

For the first time, Callie moves. She takes her eyes off the tablet, and her gaze ping-pongs from Anya to me.

"We can't hide anything from anyone for a year. Paparazzi will be on top of you after the season. Everyone will try to figure out if you're still with the winner."

Anya nods. "Right after the season is when the media is relentless. And you have the reunion to worry about too. People are invested. The first few months, you won't have a life. Not a private one."

"I can say it didn't work with the winner. I don't need–"

"They will find out," Callie says again. "They always do. And then, it will be our pictures everywhere. Then, there will be speculation. This... It's not just my job." She looks at me finally, her eyes swarming with tears. "My family will hear what people are saying. I will never find a job in this town again. I can't help my parents with the house, I..."

A tear falls, and I squeeze my eyes shut. It's over.

There's too much on the line for her, and I'm giving her nothing concrete. I'm asking her to throw it all in the wind after just a week of sex.

In the grand scheme of things, it is what it was. Months of longing and a week of sex.

"We were living on borrowed time," Callie tells me. "I'm sorry, Sebastian."

A beat of silence goes by. I can't stop looking at her. And then Anya is talking, as if my heart isn't breaking in front of her.

"The season will continue. You'll choose Vera."

I don't care, but it's Callie's eyes that whip toward the woman with a questioning gaze.

"Screen tests say she's the favorite." Anya shrugs. "If it's all the same to him, why don't we give people what they want?"

Callie nods, agreeing with the madness. To my surprise, she licks her lip and adds, "Get that porch space with the candles for their last date. It's the most romantic of the locations."

Anya nods. "I thought the same."

I want to scream.

I don't want to have dates with anyone but Callie. I need to shout at the absurdity of this conversation. To tell the world that reality shows are a sham. To just yell my fury to the wind.

I don't do it, though. I stay there; I listen and agree with them because, after all, it's not a sham.

I fell in love during *The Final Rose.*

But I shouldn't have.

CHAPTER 19
Callie

My legs are still sore from having Sebastian between them as I watch him dating other women. That keeps happening.

At some point, my mind turns itself off. I float outside of myself, and I just go about doing my job. Mechanically.

I'm not sure if I'm doing it well, but I can't stop. If I stop, I fall.

Sebastian is having a date with his winner. No one knows she's the winner yet, but I do. Vera is the fan favorite, and she once was mine too.

Now, I hate it when she gets to sit beside him on the beautiful bench overlooking the luxurious swimming pool. I hate that she's an absolute vision in pink, that the strawberry she popped into her mouth was brought by me.

I feel dirty as I listen to their easy conversation. They get along great, and even though Sebastian looked like he was close to losing it this morning, his façade is back in place.

He has media training, after all.

Everyone is trying to make them kiss, I know that much. I

recognize the angles, the low lighting, the fact we have a reduced crew so they can feel alone.

But I'm here. I'm supposed to start interviews with Maya and Abby in thirty minutes, but until then, I'm watching this.

I know this is self-harm. I'm staying here and punishing myself.

I forgot it's not just about this job. It's about any job after this. It's how the public will react to the news. It's how my face will be everywhere and what rumors will reach my parents and my brothers.

"What would you do for love?"

The question comes through my earpiece since we're a respectable distance from the couple.

Sebastian's raspy chuckle burns my insides. *"A loaded question."*

"You know I like to shoot straight. We are always talking about love..." She lets the end of the sentence linger.

"You mean a big gesture?"

I almost groan. I love his accent. At times, it's so thick, so delicious, I have to hold myself so I don't tremble.

"I guess I just want to know how fiercely you can love."

And then, I feel his eyes on me. During this whole date, he didn't dare glance my way, but he does now. His blue eyes pin me in place, and the hair on the back of my neck stands at attention. I swallow dry.

His voice fills all the gaps of my being. Suddenly, it's like he's there with me, his body over mine, his voice in the shallow of my ear. His hands on me, his promises making me believe.

"I love fiercely." A pause. *"I'll never give up on love."*

Love.

I feel like he spelled out the word for me, and I can't anymore. I take the earpiece off, turn on my heels, and leave. I don't bother to tell anyone. I can't torture myself anymore.

Inside the mansion, I'm out of myself. I can't find a place

to be alone, and I'm going to cry at any moment. I check my watch. I only have ten minutes until Maya's interview.

Cursing under my breath, I arrive in the kitchen and put my hands over the cold marble counter, breathing deep to hold the tears back.

It's done, I tell myself over and over again. We were finished back there in that room.

When I open my eyes, I'm still shaking. I'm still in the mansion, and nothing will ever change. I blink the tears away, refusing to have a meltdown on set.

A glass of water slides into my field of vision. I blink and look up at the person who got it for me.

Anya.

She nods toward the glass. I take a sip quickly as she watches. My breathing slows, and I hold her gaze, her presence keeping me grounded.

After a full minute of silence, she starts. "It's for the best."

"I know."

"Vanessa and the showrunner? She's risking a lot," she says with a frown. "It's never them. It's always on us if something goes wrong."

"I know." I nod. "I know no one would ever forgive me. The network. The fans."

"We're all human. Don't you think I don't know that? But in this industry, we need to have thick skin. You have a bright future ahead of you, and I will fight for it even when you don't want me to."

I'm holding back tears again. "Thank you. I know you're trying to protect me."

"I'm not trying. I'm *doing* it. You deserve to be on top. And you'll get there."

There's a fire in her, and I believe it. She wants me to get there; she wants to protect my career above all else, and I can only be so grateful.

"You'll go home now," she says next.

"What?"

Anya is firm. "You can't handle this, Callie. It's not even fair for me to ask you to do such a thing. I couldn't ask you to leave today because I didn't want anyone to think you did something wrong. Tomorrow, I will tell them you had a family emergency and you're out for the rest of the shooting."

I'm shaking my head already. "Anya, I can't—"

"Callie, I'm being rational when I tell you to keep away from him, but I can't make a robot out of you. Go home. Be with your family and come back next season."

I can't argue with her. It's torture. Every second away from him, every shot of him with the girls, is an arrow through my heart. This mansion. His smile. His voice in my earpiece.

I nod, agreeing.

I move, knowing that as soon as I get away from here, the better my chances not to make a scene. I make for the front entrance, and Anya comes with me, her eyes showing something soft I'm not used to seeing from her.

"I'm sorry love hurts so bad."

The words fail me. So, I simply nod and leave *The Final Rose*.

CHAPTER 20
Sebastian

"Was it you?"

I don't tread as lightly as I should. My tone is low because it's weighted with grief and defiance rather than because I'm afraid of being caught.

I don't let Vera answer. I shoulder my way to the bedroom she shares with the other finalists. Maya and Abby are in the pool, the cameras on top of them. That's why I chose this moment to find Vera.

"Was it me what?"

My breathing comes out choppy. I fight the impulse to rake my hand through my hair. I have a solo interview in twenty minutes.

"They have a video... They... Anya called Callie and I..."

I hear the door closing while I pace the bedroom from one side to the other.

"Sebastian, I don't know what you're talking about. You need to calm down and–"

I turn, my finger pointing to her face. "You were the only one who knew about Callie. No one else knew."

"You think I outed you?"

"I don't know what to think anymore, Vera."

"Well, stop being an ass, and maybe I can help," she huffs.

My fingers find my eyes, and I do my best not to remove them. I held it together the whole day after our conversation with Anya, thinking of talking to Callie in private and finding a solution. But last night, after my date with Vera, Callie wasn't anywhere to be found.

I asked a few assistants, and they all said Callie had a family emergency and left early. For a full hour, I blew up her phone, worried something happened with her parents.

I don't believe that anymore. Callie never answered my calls or replied to my texts, and today, people are saying she's out for the rest of the season.

I know in my bones they made Callie leave. We're through. She's done with me.

"Someone filmed Callie and I on the plane. Anya had a video."

Vera's hand comes to her mouth as her eyes widen. "Oh, God. How is Callie?"

My mouth opens and closes. I can't answer, because I don't know.

"She left, Vera. She's gone."

"What do you mean she's gone?"

I'm back pacing, the weight piercing my chest. "She's gone for the season. She's not answering my calls. I don't know what to do."

"God, Sebastian, sit down. You're making me dizzy."

I, for an unfathomable reason, obey her. My body sags into one of the single beds, not sure whose. Vera sits in another, right across from me, and that's the first time I look at her properly.

She has a frown right in the middle of her forehead, eyes shining with obvious concern. I know it wasn't Vera. When she knocked on my door telling me she knew about Callie, it wasn't to judge. She came to me as a friend. The conversation we had was about how I found Callie, how we became so close.

"From the beginning. What happened?" she asks in a low voice laced with concern.

"We were called in yesterday morning to talk to Anya. She had a video of me and Callie on the plane, and it was obvious something was going on between us."

"What was the camera angle?"

"What?"

Vera rolls her eyes. "Where was the person who filmed it sitting?"

I stop to think about that for the first time. "From behind, but not right behind us. A little to the side..."

"Callie was sitting close to the bathroom. Maybe it was filmed in that direction?"

I raise an eyebrow. "How do you know where she was?"

"Because you were making it obvious! I noticed something was up on our way to London when you changed your seat. Then, on the way back, you found a way to be with her again. It was reckless."

I squeeze my eyes closed. I should have never risked so much just to sit with her for an hour. At the time, that one hour felt so important, but now, the excuses for my behavior fall flat.

I grew up a Riggs. Mother told me people are always watching, quietly watching and waiting for one wrong move. One slip.

And I let them feast, eyes and ears on my biggest secret. I let them feast on Callie's career while I made promises I couldn't keep.

"We're done now."

"Sebastian–"

I shake my head, defeated. "Anya didn't fire her, but she let it be clear others would not see this in a good light. She put into words all of Callie's fears. She's afraid people are going to see her badly, like she seduced me or something."

"She's not wrong." I look at her sharply, and she raises her hands. "You know they're going to put it all on Callie, not you. You'll be the irresistible man who even the crew is falling for. But Callie?"

"I know!" I can't help feeling frustrated. "I'm well aware of the stakes for her."

"I don't think you are."

"All due respect, Vera, but I can't take one more lesson about this."

A lecture right now will not help, and I need something that will. I need a magical solution to bring Callie back to me and make the overlords of *The Final Rose* happy.

"I wasn't going to lecture you," she replies with an arched eyebrow. "But all this... Everything is about the narrative, right?"

The word stings, and I add, "I'm going to choose you, by the way. You're the fan favorite."

"Oh," she squeaks. "I've never been someone's favorite."

"Congratulations."

To my surprise, Vera laughs. "You see what I'm telling you? We are the only ones who care about what's *really* going on here. They," she points out, "care about the narrative."

"And that's why we're in this mess, Vera. Because people won't care that Callie and I fell–" I hold my tongue and breathe in through my nose. "They won't care about the feelings between Callie and me. They will make this ugly. Callie will be a homewrecker. You twelve will be the victims, and I will be the heartthrob."

"And that's why we need to change the narrative."

"Change the narrative?" I ask skeptically, but Vera is smiling.

"Yes. We're going to play producer, Sebastian Riggs."

I chuckled for the first time in twenty-four horrible hours. Vera has a lot of faith, and sometimes, it's infectious. I open my mouth to ask how we're going to play this game when the bedroom door opens.

I fly off the bed as Maya and Abby arrive. "Um, girls, I just came to talk to Vera–" I scramble to find an excuse.

"Thank God you're both here." Abby closes the door behind them.

"We don't have much time. They're coming for you soon, Sebastian."

"Coming for me?" I ask, frowning.

The two girls look at Vera, and I don't understand what's happening.

"Abby just heard from Devi," Maya explains. "Someone blabbed. They know."

The icy feeling goes down my spine. My dry mouth finds a way to ask, "About what?"

Abby looks at me like I'm insane. "You and Callie!"

I look at Vera, and she lifts a shoulder. "I said I didn't tell Anya, but I had to tell the girls. It was only right for them to know."

I don't have time to think that we four are supposedly dating just to fulfill a contract. Maya is talking fast. "The entire crew is on high alert. Adam Cork got the tip before it all blew to the wind. I don't know if he can do anything about it."

I falter. Adam Cork? The fucking showrunner knows?

"Sebastian, you don't get it," Abby says with a gulp. "Everyone knows."

"Everyone who?" I ask again, because it can't be true.

"The entire country. And whoever else watches–"

"I don't understand." I shake my head, interrupting her. "The season hasn't even aired."

"The good news is that I don't think they have Callie's name," Maya says, ignoring my line of questioning. "Devi said someone from the crew was having an affair with you. He never used Callie's name. I don't know if that means Adam Cork is putting a lid on it—"

"Since when are you so close to Devi?" I shake my head. I have no idea why it matters right now, but my brain is scrambled as it is.

"Abby is," Maya replies, as if it answers all my questions. "The season will fail before it's even on the air. They all—"

She doesn't have time to finish, though. Anya bursts into the bedroom, her eyes fixed on me.

"Riggs, with me."

CHAPTER 21
Callie

I drink wine with a straw, and it's not even the most pathetic thing that happened this week.

Three days ago, I told myself I was smart, strong, and independent. I put on my big girl pants and was set to use my time off wisely, doing arts and crafts or something like that.

Knitting for orphan kittens.

Painting my crappy apartment.

Anything and everything. I put jeans on even though I wasn't planning to leave the house, but it was one text that crushed it all. One small, five-letter text that took the floor off my feet.

Anya: I tried my best, kid.

I know what she means the second I read it. The air leaves my lungs in a hurry, and a shiver goes down my spine as I sit on my couch and turn on the TV.

I never turned my nose to the gossip channels. I can't, given my line of work. Gossip and reality TV work hand in hand. But I never thought I was going to see the day when I feared it, when I turn it on and see my biggest fear live and in color right in front of me.

"*Trouble in Paradise?*" Alison Mack, the host, says with a sadistic smile. "*The twelfth season of The Final Rose is days from airing its first episode, but rumor has it, it wasn't just the twelve hopeful hearts the new Eligible stole.*"

I hold my breath as old footage of Sebastian pops up on the screen, in one of his suits, talking in front of a children's hospital ribbon-cutting event. Clips play on a loop as Alison's voice tells the sordid tale.

"*The Final Rose's new Eligible is none other but Sebastian Riggs, Britain's most eligible bachelor. The production of The Final Rose is left scratching their heads, trying to find a way to solve this unprecedented problem. An informant says that The Final Rose is in crisis after Riggs was allegedly found having an affair with a member of the crew.*"

"*... No one can blame a girl for falling in love with Sebastian's charm, but the question needs to be asked: Is The Final Rose done? Are the contestants going to let this betrayal slide?*"

Alison Mack has a little more to say, and none of it is flattering. From there, it all goes down in flames. The internet explodes. The magazines won't dare print anything else for the days to come.

They don't have my name, but it doesn't really matter. I know it's me. I understand the joke more than the rest of Los Angeles.

So now, I watch *Friends* reruns and drink wine from a straw. I refuse to pretend I can do anything to stop this. It's out there. The world is on fire, so why not sit back and enjoy it?

So that's what I've been doing. Accepting things. One can even think I am growing from it. I'll come out of it better or whatever. But for now, I drink from my straw and avoid the first three episodes released to the streaming service.

Anytime I feel like I should have a look at the magazines, I just drink more wine and watch one more episode of *Friends*.

And right when I'm floating in self-pity—since I refuse to drown—my doorbell rings.

I don't care. One, because I'm half dressed. My old T-shirt has a stain—I'm not sure from what—and there's definitely Dorito dust on my hair. Also, it's raining.

"It's raining. Go away," I murmur to myself.

It's a storm out there, and whoever had the indecency to knock at my door needs to move on. I wouldn't open the door anyway, but the fact we're in the middle of a storm should be reason enough for people not to visit.

I flick through the channels, tired of *Friends* and find *The Big Bang Theory*. I watch it because laugh tracks are my new best friends. Whoever is downstairs rings the doorbell twice. I ignore it. I don't have a working intercom, anyway. When they suddenly go quiet, I celebrate the small victory and sink further into my stain-riddled life.

That's when the knocks on my door start. Startled, eyes wide, I just stare at the door while it jumps from its hinges.

They knock again, and this time, accompanied by a familiar voice—the last voice I wanted to hear right now.

"Open up, Callie!"

I close my eyes in a prayer.

Dear God, if you make this a bad dream, I promise to be extra good. I'll light candles with Mami and Abuelita for Abuelo's soul. I'll do other things good Colombian girls ought to do.

But the door jumps again with the force of his fist, and with a groan, I open it in one painless move.

He brushes the wet hair off his face, looking me up and down with the sort of mockery I hate so much.

"You look like shit, Callie."

"Thank you for your visit. You can go now."

My brother simply arches an eyebrow at me and comes inside, wet and all, his work boots dragging water all over my floors. He goes to find a towel for himself as I stay there, holding the door open. After all, where Dario goes, so does Ben.

"He's parking the truck," Dario informs me while drying his hair.

"Where?" I shake my head.

"Away from this horrible neighborhood, Callie. We aren't stupid. You live in a place we don't even trust to park the truck."

"How dramatic of you." I let the door go, and it closes at once.

Dario stands there, watching me. He was a lanky kid growing up, always skinny and getting himself into trouble. It was only when he started working with Ben that he got the muscles he shows off now. The eyes are the same, though, of a bold kid waiting his turn to cause mayhem.

I love my brothers, but I don't want them here to watch me swim in self-pity.

"Is it you?"

I ignore the question, burying myself on the couch and turning the volume up for a queued laugh track.

"Callie, come on."

"Don't sit anywhere. You're all wet," I say, my nose upright like I'm the Queen of England.

"Oh sure, in this palace? No way. You should live with Mom. It's safer."

"Mom already has you and Ben mooching off her. I'm the good kid."

Dario laughs. "Ben is the good kid."

I lift my shoulder. "At least I left."

He opens his mouth to reply something ridiculous, I'm sure, but that's when Ben chooses to arrive without knocking, just coming inside like he owns the damn place.

"I parked ten minutes away because you live in a hellhole, Calliope."

"Fuck you," I reply, looking at the TV and ignoring my big brother.

Ben doesn't pay attention to my words and turns to Dario. He's wet too, but he doesn't seem to mind that much.

"Is it her?"

"She won't tell," Dario states. "But she looks like shit. It's probably her."

"I'll be very grateful if you two would stop talking about me like I'm not sitting right here."

Ben takes a chair from my improvised kitchen set and drags it to sit beside me on the couch. With one simple move, he maneuvers himself over it with open legs, resting on his elbows on his knees.

"How come he's allowed to sit?" Dario whines.

"I didn't invite him to," I growl.

Ben raises his palm to end the argument, and my tongue gets stuck in the roof of my mouth. Damn, I hate it when he does that. It's an old move of his to finish our endless arguments. One flick of his wrist, and the words die on the tip of my tongue.

"Callie. The news. Are they telling the truth?"

"I wouldn't know what you're talking about."

Ben sighs, and helpfully, Dario turns my TV off.

"I'm going to ask again, Callie," Ben explains calmly, "and I need you to think hard about what answer you're going to give me."

Before he has a chance to ask, I whip my head toward him, fury in my eyes. "Why does that even matter?"

"It matters because we are going to kill Sebastian Riggs, aren't we?" Dario replies, searching Ben for confirmation, like murder is a common topic in the Sosa household.

"You're not killing Sebastian," I say before I can stop myself.

"HA!" Dario jumps, his finger pointed at me. "So it is you!"

"I think you both should go. I have things to do."

"Can we be serious for a second?" Ben starts again. "How much trouble are you in? Were you fired?"

And there's so much concern in his voice, I can't fight anymore. I'm embarrassed, but some things are more important than that.

I shake my head. "Anya just asked me to step away until they finish shooting this season. Do Mom and Dad know?"

Ben shakes his head quickly. "She's dying to call to see if you can blab the name."

I let out a breath. "God bless her."

"Can you tell us what happened now?" Dario asks, finally grabbing a chair and sitting on my other side.

I wish the TV was still on so I could fix my eyes there. It's not, so I just let my eyes wander as they gather tears.

"I thought you heard the news."

"We heard the shit version of it."

"That Sebastian is so handsome, not even the hussy field producer could resist?" I can't stop the pathetic sniffle.

"Yes, those were the exact words," Ben says dryly. "What happened?"

I turn and give him a watery smile. "I liked him and he liked me. We lied to ourselves that there was a way out of the mess, and then...there wasn't."

"Did he do anything he shouldn't?" Ben needs to know.

I shake my head. "Sebastian Riggs never does things he shouldn't do. Until me, I guess."

Dario gags theatrically. "Let's try not to talk about him doing you, please."

"That wasn't what I meant!"

"Sure." He grimaces. "But he likes you too. So, why are

you dressed like a homeless woman with a lifetime supply of Doritos?" He points at me up and down.

"I'm not–" I can't even defend my attire. "It's hopeless, alright? Sebastian has a contract with the network, which means he'll need to choose one of the girls. Until the season is over, he can't announce or be seen with anyone. And after..."

"It will look like you sabotaged your own show." Ben gets it, nodding and gazing at me with pity.

"Well, that's bullshit!" Of course, Dario rages. "He went to the damn show, and he fell in love, didn't he? That's *literally* the premise!"

I ignore the word *love* floating above us. I can't think about it right now, and I know it doesn't matter. If I sit here and accept I love Sebastian Riggs, it will make things much worse.

And just because I can't, because it makes everything harder, this is the moment when I realize how much I love Sebastian Riggs.

Colorful cursing streams from my mouth, making Dario hoot and Ben watch me with wariness.

"He needs to choose from the twelve," I finally say.

"Can't you date in secret for a while?" Dario wants to know, and Ben slices him with a look. My younger brother lifts his hands under Ben's frown. "Hey, it's not like I'm suggesting for her to be a dirty little–"

"Callie won't be anyone's secret," Ben decrees.

A faint start of a smile comes to my lips. "Not for all the honorable reasons Ben is thinking about. But that wouldn't work." I sigh. "The press will be on top of Sebastian for months to come. All they want to know is if he's still with the winner. It's asking to be caught."

For a couple of minutes, the Sosa children stare at nothing. I hate how well I explained this predicament. I wait for Dario to shout another silly suggestion, or for Ben to give me an honorable solution. I stay there, wrapped in hope, waiting for my brothers to come up with a way out, but they never do.

It's not that I haven't thought of leaving it all behind and setting my career on fire. In the days since I saw Sebastian last, it was all I thought about. I could give everything up because, at the end of the day, what I really want is to be happy.

Sebastian became an important part of my happiness, that much I can't deny. But I'm a whole person. I need my family, my friends, my hobbies, my silly ways to entertain myself and I need my career, too. I can't leave it all behind and expect it to work between us.

We need to be two distinct people who want to be together, but if I self-destruct, what's left of me to love him?

"Come home with us," Ben begs.

I'm already shaking my head, but he interrupts me. "You're hurt. Your place is home."

And he's right. I'm not doing myself any favors by staying away. I need my family right now, more than ever.

The storm outside has passed finally, and I go to my room to pack a bag. Dario suggests I take a shower, and while I flip him off, I know he's right. Mom is going to skin me alive if she sees me in this state.

They drive me home afterward. I sit between them on the truck bench, feeling small as Ben negotiates the streets to our old and reliable neighborhood.

The sun is shining when Ben parks in front of our house, erasing any memories of the storm we left behind. I leave my bag for them and open the small gate at the front. Mom's flowers are to my left. Dad is a gardener. He insists on pristine flowers but says they are all for Mom.

Instead of going through the house, I keep to the little pathway to the backyard. As I turn the corner, I see big, colorful sheets hung to dry in the unexpected sun. They dance with the breeze, and I hear Mom's humming.

She has a basket of wet clothes beside her knees, a bunch of pegs secured to an apron as she fixes the clothes on the washing line.

I smile when she sees me. Dad's shirt in her hands never makes it to the line. A huge smile splits her face. Age lines in the corner of her eyes are the only proof the years have passed.

"*Mija*," she sighs. "You're home."

And I go to her. Thank God I'm home.

CHAPTER 22

Callie

"Don't you dare take those boots off, Dario!" I warn, pointing at his hands hovering over the laces of said boots.

"Excuse me? I can't wear my work boots at home!"

"They will stink up the whole house!" I gasp, but he's already doing it.

Weeks of living at home only proved that children should leave their parents' house. Mom fed me more than was necessary while she checked my forehead like I was truly sick. She called me pale and fed me *ajiaco*, but since I refused to tell her the truth, my mysterious illness persisted.

I *feel* sick. I need a reason to be parked on her couch, arguing with Dario like we're teenagers again, and sickness is the perfect answer to all my prayers.

"Oh, God!" I gag once the boots are removed. "I'm telling Dad on you!" I screech, taking my blanket with me when I remove myself from my seat.

"It's a gazillion degrees outside, Callie," Dario points out, bringing his foot up on the coffee table.

"Thanks for the weather report, pinhead."

"Why the hell are you walking around like a burn victim with that blanket?"

Mom comes from the kitchen to save me, her gaze loving. Her cool palm checks my forehead once more in such a soothing motion, I almost purr.

"Language, Dario. Callie is under the weather." Mom fusses.

"I wonder what she has." Dario crosses his arms over his chest. "Such a long recovery."

"No feet on my furniture!" To no one's surprise, Mom slaps his smelly feet off the table, and I make a face of victory at him.

Maybe I have regressed a little since coming back home, but I need all the love and attention Mom is always ready to give. I need the afternoons when Dad is back from work and we play chess while he tells me long-winded stories about trees.

It's...perfect.

I want to be coddled and called by my childhood nickname. I want to feel protected and forget that *The Final Rose* ever—

"Put the TV on," are Ben's first words when he arrives home, Dad trailing after him.

"Gladly." Dario is quick to oblige, turning the TV right on.

"You've got to be fucking kidding me!" I sneer.

"Language!" the other four Sosas say, and I narrow my eyes to my brothers.

Dario is always a couple of minutes early, coming in and annoying the life of me. Then, there's Ben, usually the last person at the construction site. Right now, their project is near where Dad is working, so both trucks arrive at the same time most nights.

Usually, Dario annoys me and tries to steal food while

Mom is distracted asking Dad about his day, and that's when Ben disappears for a shower.

But no one is moving today. Dad comes over to give Mom a kiss, and I get one on my temple while I stand still, watching my idiot brothers with narrowed eyes.

The TV is paused in *The Final Rose's* logo, and I can't help but wince. This is what I wanted to avoid.

The season finale.

Maya, Abby, or Vera. Who cares? *It's not me.*

"Dario, maybe we should turn the TV off?" Dad asks with his gentle voice.

"Turn it off, dick face," I tell him from gritted teeth.

"Now, Calliope, no name-calling," Mom chimes in with an edge of warning in her voice. "But turn the television off, Dario."

Dario smiles at me the same way he smiled when I caught him trying pot when he was fifteen: an unperturbed, cheerful smile. Either my little brother is the most relaxed person on Earth or a psychotic murderer.

Right now, I'm the one ready to start the murdering spree.

Straight to the offensive, I leave my blanket behind and leap to the couch, reaching for the remote. Dario yelps, scrambling to hide it from me as Dad tells us to stop and Mom threatens to get us with a flip-flop.

I don't hear any of my family. My heart is leaping out of my chest, my breathing coming out in hurtful puffs. I'm not ready to see it. I'm not ready to hear Sebastian's voice and sit there while he chooses the path of his heart.

During the weeks we've been apart, I've been telling myself the results wouldn't matter. Anya decided he was going to choose Vera since she's the fan favorite. Even though, I know it isn't really Sebastian's choosing, my irrational heart can't take it.

Reality is what we construct. Nothing is real until we

make it so, and that's what we do on reality TV. We distort the truth; we build around it and create whatever we want until truth and lies are so woven together, it's impossible to tell them apart.

And that's when the lies become true too, because enough people believe in it.

I hold back tears, inches from scratching Dario's face off. "Give me that remote, you turd!"

"Enough!" Mom's voice cuts through. "Can't you see your sister is suffering?"

My arm stops mid-action.

No, I'm sick.

I've been mysteriously sick for weeks, and that's why I need her cuddles and food, why I walk around with a blanket around my shoulders.

"I'm sick," I say in the smallest voice.

"You're heartbroken, baby," Mom says, and I wince.

I don't want to be heartbroken. I'm Callie Fucking Sosa. I'm a beast on the set. I'm all focused, and I'm unstoppable. I don't lose my mind because of stupid things like my heart.

"I'm sick, Mami," I tell her again, my eyes shining in her direction, borderline pathetic.

Mom opens her mouth to say something else, but my dad stops her before the words are even formed. She holds her tongue back, and the four of them stare down at me, saying nothing and everything at the same time.

They can see my bleeding heart through my lies, and I'm filled with shame.

I get off Dario, ignoring his sigh of relief. I sit beside him with a sniffle as Dad, that saint of a man, gets my blanket from the ground and puts it back around my shoulders.

"No one is trying to be cruel to you, Callie," Ben speaks for the first time since ordering the TV on.

He stands by the door, eyes locked on mine. Ben is tall and

big, has always been too big for his own good. He's my big brother, and I always thought he was bigger than life itself.

He defended me and Dario our whole lives. He never let us go astray. His eyes pin me in place, and my heart squeezes. I don't want to hear what he has to say. I don't care what it is, I'm going to ig—"

"You need to watch this. Do you trust me?"

I want to cry, but I nod instead.

Ben lets out a breath, and Dario readjusts beside me. Mom and Dad, who until now were frozen by the kitchen's door, finally move to sit on my left side.

I hold my tongue so I don't question what kind of shock therapy this is.

Dario presses play. *The Final Rose's* theme song starts, and I gulp.

"In the last episode of The Final Rose..." Fox's voiceover announces, but Dario stops right on a zoom in of Sebastian's face.

"We don't need the recap... No..." Dario murmurs to himself, skipping ahead to the actual episode.

That was it, wasn't it? I saw Sebastian's face, and I didn't burst into flames or tears or become a pile of salt or something. No. I'm still here, in my parents' home, nursing a broken heart, my lip quivering like life itself is taking turns hitting me in the ribs.

But the thing is, I'm still alive.

That's why they make breakup songs saying as much. Because we do—we survive. It doesn't matter how much it hurts and how many pieces you're in afterward.

We are more than that. I'm more than that.

"Ready?" I'm taken by surprise by Dario's question.

I turn to him, nodding. Ready.

He points the remote at the TV.

Here we go.

Goosebumps rise on my skin, even with the blanket over my shoulders. The words coming from *The Final Rose's* host make little sense to me. She talks about an unforgettable season, twists and turns, and true love. It's the first season I haven't watched every episode religiously. Nessa and I always watch the first episode together while we joke around and check TV apps to spy on the public's favorites.

"And here come our hopefuls..." Andrea Fox calls. *"Maya Denver."*

I hold my breath when the camera pans to her. She's a vision in purple, her mouth in a perfect smile. Maya had enough potential to be the season's main girl. She's shy, honest, funny, and just the right amount of nerdy. I give her a month before she's snagged by someone else.

"Vera Kaur."

I gasp with the rest of my family when it's Vera's turn. Her color is emerald green, that much is obvious. At this point, the color is her brand, and I'll forever associate it with her. The dress is perfect, with a daring neckline, her hair gathered over her shoulder, cascading in caramel waves.

She's the winner, and she looks like it.

I mean, I knew she was, but now, as she walks down the stairs and chats with Alison, I can see it in her posture.

It's her show. This is her moment.

I'm supposed to be happy to see a finale with so many genuine and amazing people. I should be watching it with the crew over cocktails, relieved it's over and excited for next season.

Happiness is the last thing I feel. My hands shake, and a single lonely, pathetic tear falls. I sniffle without meaning to, and one hand reaches for mine at my left, another at my right.

Left, Mom.

Right, Dario.

I nod to reassure them I'm ok, but they never let my hands

go. We watch in weighted silence as Abby comes along in a romantic pink number. With the three of them finally there, all I want is to scream.

I never felt as bad about myself as I feel right now. I feel empty, like I lack something.

And that something might be courage.

"This season would not be the same if it wasn't for him. The man this side of the ocean fell in love with. Sebastian Riggs."

I want to weep.

I would say he looks flawless, but the word lost its meaning. The blue suit matches his eyes. The coy smile breaks my heart. He goes down the stairs in obscene slow motion. The camera pans up his perfect shoes, up his legs, the expanse of his chest as he fixes the cufflinks, rehearsed moves like the footage from the teaser.

I yelp like a lost puppy, and Mom's hand squeezes mine. I'm being dramatic, but I can't help it. If staying in this house taught me anything, it's that I can be soft when I have my support system behind me.

And I have them right now, holding my hand and not judging me in the slightest. I smile a watery smile at my mom, and she kisses me on the cheek.

The next leg of the show features clips of the cast being funny. The many times Abby said the word "vegan", all the times Maya tripped or Vera talked too fast. And then...Sebastian. They show clips of him being his British self, the words he used that made the cast and crew stop for a second.

Even I have to laugh at some of them. I used to keep a list on my phone of my favorite sayings of his, but since I left the mansion, I didn't have the heart to look at it again.

I always loved this part of the show, when the raw footage was shown. It was Jeff's decision to add it in season seven, and I think it's honestly the best addition for the show.

The footage isn't always picture-perfect, like the rest of the episodes. It shows us in the background, a rogue boom coming to a scene when someone laughs too hard. But it's always a nice sample of how the show is made.

By real people.

I'm honestly having fun when the music changes, and I almost forget to be nervous. I remind myself I have no reason to be. I know he'll pick Vera. I was there when it was decided.

And yet, I tremble and suck in a breath.

"You know what's coming, Sebastian?" Alison asks good-naturedly. *"You know I have to ask..."*

This is wrong.

It's too early in the episode. *"Who has the final rose?"* comes much later. It's the last thing on the show. The finale usually drags, giving them time to talk and mislead the public.

"What—" I start, but Dario, of all people, shushes me.

I turn to him with a frown, but I don't have time for my brother.

"Who has the final rose?" Alison asks, and I hold my breath.

The camera zooms in on Sebastian, and he looks straight ahead.

"From the moment I signed up for The Final Rose, *I knew that would be a hard question to answer. I've met so many incredible women in the last months..."*

The screen shows the three girls smiling at him.

"I made so many friends, but I came here to fall in love. And the thing is...I did."

The image changes, and it's not footage of the mansion during the season finale anymore.

The footage is of *us*.

I dart upright, my eyes widening when I see myself on TV. I'm in the background, my hair a mess on top of my head, dressed in my *The Final Rose* tee and shorts. The camera zooms in. I can't hear what we're saying, but it's clear we're laughing.

"I came into this experience with an open heart, ready for it to take me in any direction," says his voiceover. *"Again and again, life proves love is never predictable."*

The footage is endless. We are at the mini-golf course, laughing as I fix his tie.

We walk through the set, clearly arguing, my hands moving in all directions as he makes a face.

Sebastian's saying something silly on camera, but it pans to me, and I'm laughing, holding my earpiece.

I'm sleeping with my head on his shoulder on an airplane.

"I know everyone is invested in this show. I'm truly grateful for the fans and all the support you have given The Final Rose, *so that's why I chose to tell the truth. This is real. I'm a real man who fell in love on a reality TV show."*

The bastard pulls on all my heartstrings, and I make a sound that isn't human. I feel myself shaking, having an out-of-body experience.

"It wasn't like I thought it was going to be, but life hardly is. I know this isn't the finale you all wanted, but I'm asking you to bear with me and let me talk to the girl who stole my heart when she wasn't even trying."

The screen flickers to England. It's night, and no one can even make out the silhouettes of our bodies, but it's clear when we kiss. I hold my breath, not sure how to react. I'm kissing on camera, but before I even react, Sebastian is back on the screen.

"Love, I know you never wanted something like this, but we deserve a grand finale. You taught me how to be unapologetically truthful, and this is what I'm doing."

I only realize I'm crying because Mom grips my shoulder and asks me not to. I hold my words in my mouth with a shaky hand.

"You're the only one for me, Callie. Hands down, you're the one with the final rose."

For the first time in all eleven years of *The Final Rose*, the episode ends suddenly. It fades out, and lettering appears.

"Sebastian Riggs will wait for his chosen one at the mansion."

I gasp and stand, the blanket falling from my shoulders as more lettering appears.

"Until she comes."

"Oh, my God!" It's the first thing I've said since the episode started.

It ends like always, with a line of credits and an upbeat song, but I'm rooted to the spot. I can't move a muscle until a jingle of keys interrupts my thoughts.

Ben is over to the side, throwing his car keys in the air and grabbing them with ease. He smirks at me. "I drive."

"Great, let's go." Dario unfolds from the couch, stretching his body.

"I...I–" I stutter.

But Mom grabs my arm and turns me toward her and Dad.

"You have to go." She's firm.

I want to ask if she's disappointed, if she thinks it was wrong to let all that happen between Sebastian and me. She doesn't let me talk, though.

"He sounds like he really loves you."

Dad huffs, shaking his head. "Of course he does! What's not to love? She's Calliope Sosa."

I don't tell Dad it's Sebastian's name that's the famous one, that *he* is the one who just had twelve women competing for his heart, that he has more money than any of us can understand. I don't say any of it, because he's right.

What's not to love?

"Let's go, Callie. Traffic will be a bitch if we wait much longer." Dario is hurrying me along.

"Language, Dario," Mom tries just one more time.

"Mom, this is an extraordinary event!" he argues. "Don't you get it? Callie is going to marry a millionaire! If I don't get to swear now, when can I do it?"

"You can never swear," Mom deadpans, and my brother, honest to God, huffs and whines.

I put my sneakers on and pull my hair into a ponytail while ignoring everything around me. In less than a minute, I'm out the door, Ben on my heels. I practically jog to the car and try to suppress my annoyance when Dario slides me to the middle of the bench.

"Do you need to come?"

He scoffs. "Of course!"

I'm going to reply, but Ben is already driving off. I wish we could go faster. I wish we could fly down the streets. My leg bounces nervously, and Dario smacks it.

"Tell us what you're going to say to him." Before I can tell him I don't know, he interrupts me. "Unless it's dirty. Don't tell us then."

Ben growls, which might mean he also doesn't want to know.

"It's not like I have a speech prepared."

We stop in traffic, and Ben looks at the road ahead. "You have a couple of hours to figure it out."

CHAPTER 23

Sebastian

I look at the endless grass in front of me and take a deep breath, legs bent, arms straight, leaning on the golf club. I sway, testing the position, and then I look far ahead to the flag.

Swing, hit, and I watch as the ball soars through the air in a graceless arch.

Bollocks.

I was never a good golfer. And I'm just as bad at mini-golf.

"She'll come," someone says behind me, and I don't need to turn my head to see who.

The woman is many things, and most of them annoy me. I have to respect her, though; I know she cares about Callie first and foremost. Still, Anya and I will never be best mates.

"I know she will," I say, taking a moment before looking at the woman.

"But you've been looking like a wounded puppy since we came back."

We returned two days ago when the finale aired. I stayed in my hotel room like a good boy. I gave nothing to the press. I played the game like they told me to. On the morning of the season finale, I returned to the mansion and watched the episode with a few crew members who agreed to stay until Callie came back.

Two days later, we're still here.

Two days of watching every car down the street, holding my breath each passing hour.

Forty-eight hours of hell.

I know she'll come for me. I know her brothers are going to make her watch it, and if they don't...she'll know what's going on eventually.

The Callie Vigil is impossible to miss. The internet is on fire; *#WhereIsShe* has been trending since the finale aired. The street is lined with paparazzi night and day.

The whole damn town is holding its breath, waiting for Callie, and I'm terrified. I gambled big when I said yes to this. Vera was certain this was the way to go. She wanted the public to know that reality was better than fiction, but I wasn't so sure how Callie would feel.

When someone tipped off the press that we were together, this became about more than just Callie's job. Adam Cork got involved, and it was obvious that the network was pressuring him.

He arrived on set with a file; apparently, it wasn't hard to find out who sold the tip to the media—an intern who was promptly fired.

A sense of emptiness washed over me. It wasn't satisfying enough. I was hurting, Callie was hurting, and I wanted to see that intern crumble under the weight of the consequences of his actions.

Vera steered me back to the right path. "This is not the story. It's not about revenge. It's about love".

As each episode aired, the whispers grew. Everyone knew what was happening, and they were watching the show for a chance to see a producer in the background.

Whether she wanted to be or not, Callie was part of this season, even if her face wasn't on screen.

Little by little, Adam Cork and Anya were convinced of Vera's plan. Telling the truth wasn't just good for the soul anymore; it was good television.

The casting director got involved and pulled footage of me and Callie. Apparently, a cameraman liked to film the crew and give everyone a little end-of-the-season gift.

Once on the screen, there was no denying it.

Callie and I are magic together.

Cork finally agreed it might be the smartest marketing strategy of the century.

I hated that he called it that, but saving the show was important to Callie too. With one move, I could save us all.

I opened my heart during that episode. It wasn't a perfect ending, wasn't pure and off-camera, but it was ours, and it was true.

I fell in love on *The Final Rose,* and I was waiting for her to come to me. While the wait was torturous, I'd wait a thousand days for her.

I might as well get good at mini golf as I waited.

"You know, Sebastian," Anya speaks again, "I really thought you were going to be the end."

"Of Callie or the show?"

She chuckles. "Both."

"Now you're going to tell me you were wrong? I'm a great bloke. You wished you had seen it before?" I arch an eyebrow.

She looks me right in the eyes, shaking her head. "She's here."

CHAPTER 24
Callie

"F uck!"

Ben curses, and I can only agree. We turn a corner, and instead of looking at the gorgeous scenery, in front of us is a crowd of people.

More specifically, paparazzi. They lounge in front of the mansion like it's their new hangout spot, and Ben has to step on the breaks as the three of us gape at the crowd.

I left the house with a soccer jersey, denim shorts, and a ponytail. I was thinking about how much I wanted to see Sebastian, how much I missed that stupid face of his, but I completely forgot it wasn't just me who watched the season finale.

The paparazzi spot us, and I curse when a flash burns my retinas. The first picture of me is probably of my shell-shocked expression over the dashboard.

Ben pushes the truck forward, seemingly not scared of running people over. They probably get the message from the scowl on his face and let us go, even if at snail's pace.

A man a head taller than everyone else parts the crowd like Moses, and I breathe easily when I see Antonio's familiar face.

He shoos the reporters away, a snarl on his lip, and Ben follows his directions to park in front of the mansion.

Without taking his eyes off the front door and his hands from the wheel, my older brother asks, "Are you ready?"

No.

No, I'm not ready to have my picture plastered in every shitty magazine tomorrow morning. I'm not ready to have them speculate about what Sebastian Riggs saw in a girl with a ponytail and Colombia's national team jersey.

But I'm ready to see him. I need to see him. I nod numbly.

"I'm going to open the door and help you out," Dario says. "You hold on to me, ok?"

I look up at my younger brother and try to feel secure about his words. Ben and Dario are here. Antonio is just outside, shooing people away from the passenger door.

Sebastian is inside.

"All right." I grip his arm.

Once the door is open, though, I waver. The flashlights are blinding, their voices yelling on top of each other.

"What are you going to say to him?"

"Is it true you were having an affair before this season stared?"

"What do you have to say to the contestants who fell in love with Sebastian?"

I don't answer any of their questions. I can't. I'm overwhelmed and confused. I look down and follow Dario's steps as he follows Antonio's. Ben magically appears behind me, and I hear him stopping one reporter, then another when they venture too close.

It's a short walk, but it takes forever.

They ask things repeatedly, and not all of them make sense. Not all are flattering, not all are about love. I tune them out and look down at my shoes. When I go up the two steps to the main door, I breathe in.

Dario takes my arm and hauls me through. Ben is right on my heels, and then, the noise is gone, the flashes stop, and there's finally silence.

I look up, and I see all my friends.

I stumble back, but Ben holds me by my shoulders. Around the main shooting area is a small crew, cameras, sound, and assistants, all are smiling at me. David, the cameraman, gives me a thumbs-up from behind the equipment. Doris is in the back, smiling big.

I stay frozen, looking at them, an impossibly big lump stuck in my throat.

Devi comes closer, greeting me quickly before he starts mic-ing me up. My mouth is opening and closing like I'm a fish. I let him run the wires under my clothes when Nessa comes along, her eyes full of tears.

"Just relax and don't look at the camera, ok?"

"Nessa..." I'm able to say, but that's it.

She smiles at my inability to talk. "Don't talk too fast. David and Gary are working on A and B, ok?"

I don't point out she's the one talking fast now. Devi moves behind me, hooking the mic on my shorts. Nessa is giving me the basics we run through with the first-timers. I never thought I was going to be on this side of the conversation.

My eyes must tell how scared I am, because once Devi is finished and gone, Nessa takes my hands and squeezes. My brothers aren't beside me anymore, and my heart hammers inside my chest. I wiggle my hands in front of my body, and I catch Jeff making a face. I laugh, knowing I'm ruining the shot with all my fidgeting and brushing my clothes on the mic.

I never said *I* was camera-ready.

I'm still laughing at the irony of it all when I hear steps coming from the back door. My eyes raise the second he's in the view.

The air leaves my lungs.

Sebastian Riggs.

He cuts through the small crowd, stopping in the middle of the room. He's back on his mark. Every week, he stands there to eliminate a contestant.

My wobbly legs move when he calls my name.

"Callie..."

I love the way he says it. He even makes my name sound magical.

I walk to him, and everything I practiced saying for the last couple of hours evaporates.

"What a way to get my attention."

I hear a few snickers, but my eyes are fixed on him. His blue eyes are shining, and he has a little wrinkle in the corner when he smiles.

"You know me. I like to make a scene."

"What would the King say?"

"I expect a sternly worded letter from His Majesty himself any minute now."

"What's stern-worded for royalty?"

He thinks for a second. "Unbelievably passive-aggressive."

"No," I scoff, "that's just British."

He chuckles, and I follow suit. Sebastian shakes his head, pinching the bridge of his nose. "Jesus, I'm mucking this up."

"Why? Don't you think the public wants to hear about us making fun of the King?"

With a serious face, he steps close and takes my hands. "Americans are way more sensitive about the royal family than most English I know."

"Let's talk about the probability of that being remotely true."

"Let's talk about us, Callie Sosa."

I swallow my witty comebacks. It's easy to forget everything with Sebastian. We did that once, didn't we? We forgot he was the Eligible and I was a field producer. We forgot our places and why it wasn't going to work.

And now, I forget that we're mic-ed and all my colleagues are watching.

"This is not what you imagined," he says first. "I know you never wanted to be on this side of the camera. So, I need to apologize for that first."

I open my mouth, but he shakes his head. "Me first." I make a face but shut my mouth.

His thumbs play with the skin on the top of my hand. I feel his touch from head to toe.

"All I ever wanted was to find someone who truly saw me. Beyond my last name, the suits, and the charity events. I wanted someone for me and not because I'm a Riggs. I agreed to come on *The Final Rose* because I wanted to be surprised at least once in my life." He smiles. "And boy, how surprised I was."

I bite my lip, trying not to interject as he says, "And it was there," he points to the little alcove to the right, "where I saw you for the first time. Where you said I was too sarcastic and that wouldn't work for TV. You wanted to give me a sarcasm sign."

I chuckle and I hear other people laughing, too.

"It was right there," he points toward the kitchen, "where Maverick kept sending me flowers, and you said you'd kill me if I had a girlfriend."

"Surely I said something way more colorful than that," I argue.

"Oh, you did, but they're still recording, darling."

I nod dutifully, and I can't stop the little smile on my lips.

"It was out there," he points at the back lawn, "that I asked if it was your favorite sport was making all the men in your life feel stupid."

"Yes!" Dario yells from somewhere.

Sebastian turns away from me for the first time, searching for a face among many. "Are your brothers here?"

I nod. "Yeah."

He doesn't seem to really care, his eyes on me again. "It was in this house I fell in love with you, Callie, and you know why?"

My vision blurs, and I shake my head.

"Because I fell in love when I laid my eyes on you for the first time."

I'm crying. I'm crying silently, and I don't know what to do. No one tells you what to say when the man you love says all these nice things for the first time.

But then, I remember.

"Oh, God. I love you, too!"

He chuckles a little, but a weighted breath dislodges from his chest, as if he thought for a silly second that I didn't feel the same.

"Well, that's great, because I have a question for you..."

Sebastian removes his hands from mine and lowers down onto one knee. The crew obviously doesn't give a crap anymore, because they all gasp, and I hear Ben swearing.

I place my hand in my mouth, shaking as the tears stream down my cheeks. I can't breathe. I can't think.

Sebastian grabs something from his pocket—a box.

"I knew it when I saw you for the first time. I knew it when we talked and when we joked, even when we fought. I always knew you were the person who was going to change my entire life. Calliope Sosa, will you marry me?"

I don't think I have the words. Tears pour down my face, but then a hollow sound finds its way from my lips. I can barely hear myself over the beat of my heart, but everything in me is saying the same thing.

"Yes!"

I say it again as he slides a huge ring onto my finger. I

choke it out on a cry, then as he stands and takes me in his arms.

I repeat the word in my head when we kiss, his mouth over mine, his body so perfect against mine.

I shake, I cry, and I laugh.

Sebastian Riggs finally chose.

And he chose *me*.

Epilogue

CALLIE

I hold the edge of the hot tub, my knuckles white. My legs kick, the water splashing as I curse colorfully in Spanish.

He bites my inner thigh with a chuckle. "I love that dirty mouth."

I don't have time to be a smart-ass. He's back on me, his tongue on my clit, working me sinfully and bringing me to the precipice of an orgasm.

My bikini was ripped from my body a long time ago. Sebastian said no clothing and he's taking his rule seriously.

He digs his fingers into my ass cheeks, angling me just right so he can continue to make a meal out of me. I let out a soft moan, my hands going to his hair to hold him in place.

My heart beats fast, the heat uncurling from my spine in a zing until I'm left shaking. The orgasm is powerful. I throw my head back in a gasp, and he laughs. He's always so proud of himself when I come like this.

My legs are still jelly when he hops from the hot tub and pulls me with him. Three quick steps, and he dives straight into the cold pool.

"Asshole," I say when we emerge, brushing the wet hair out of my face.

"The temperature change is good for the muscles." He smirks, and I know he's full of shit.

I lay my head on his shoulders, my legs circling his waist as he moves us around the pool in the beautiful, warm night.

"Are you ready?" I whisper.

"I was ready a year ago." He doesn't miss a beat.

He proposed to me a year ago. He wanted to get married right away, but I said no. We had time.

We needed time to be a normal couple.

We weren't normal for a long time, though. It was impossible with the press on top of us after that season finale. Things cooled off after a while, and we got to go on our first date.

He ate with my parents and got closer to my brothers. We were able to just be, and that was all I ever wanted.

Eventually, I decided it was time, and he promptly asked me where I wanted to get married.

He would marry me anywhere—London or here, big party or small.

Silly as it was, I knew where: *the mansion*.

I've never seen the mansion this time of the year; it feels odd without the cameras and hundreds of people around. Sebastian insisted on staying here a couple of days before the wedding, and now, I see why.

We're having sex in every place he imagined us doing it while he was the Eligible.

Not bad for my last day before becoming Mrs. Riggs.

His parents arrive tomorrow. We met once, and that one

time was enough. Bea is one of my bridesmaids, along with Nessa and Doris.

Most of the crew is invited, and I know it's going to be weird for all of us, but kind of amazing too.

Sebastian twirls us in the water, the movement painting shapes in the pool. We hold each other for a long time, breathing in the calm before the madness.

We were born in the madness, so we aren't so scared.

"When did you know you loved me?" I ask.

He holds me closer, kissing my hair. "When I saw you through the mirror that first day. I thought you were the most beautiful woman in the world."

I giggle. "No, really."

He takes a second to reply this time. "It wasn't just one moment, but all of them. I fell in love with each part of you, and I'm still falling. Every day, I'm thankful I get to fall in love with you again."

I sniff. "Jesus, Riggs, save it for the vows."

He chuckles, and we go silent again. Wiping away a silly tear with the back of my hand, I move onto his lap. My hands go to his face, feeling the delicious stubble that tells me he hasn't shaved in a couple of days.

"Thanks for choosing me, Riggs," I whisper.

"Always," replies America's most eligible man.

Tomorrow, he will be my husband.

If you like this book please consider leaving a review.

If you want to read more from me, why don't try Keepsake?

· · ·

Angsty, full of heat and heart. I'll make you cry.
Available on Kindle Unlimited, paperback and audio.

Author's note

Thank you so much for reading *The Final Rose*.

This book was published initially two years ago under a different title and cover. It flopped. HARD. I couldn't even get my loyal readers to pick it up, and I was confused as to why.

But I was too unwell to investigate. My dad had just passed, and I took it as another thing going on. A month ago, I made a post saying I loved the story, but I never really understood why it didn't take off, that sometimes, it's not meant to be.

Well, people didn't agree with me.

They loved the premise, and I got not only comments, but messages from plenty of readers asking about the book.

So, I decided to give it another chance. I retitled it, got a new cover, and opened an ARC form. I also lit a candle and prayed it was finally time.

I'm not going to lie, I'm scared. I'm putting myself out there and hoping not to fail.

I hope it's time for Callie and Sebastian, so if you liked this book, please help me spread the word.

We wouldn't be here if wasn't for a few people.

Santana Knox, who came up with the title *The Final Rose* and once again made magic with my shitty blurb.

Aurelia Knight, who held my hand while I freaked out and edited a lot of last-minute scenes.

Connie from Bella Books, my proofreader and favorite cheerleader.

Alexa Thomas, my editor who jumped into this to help this story shine.

And my husband, who patiently took over chores and looking after our nine-month-old so I could give this book the love it deserved.

Thank you all.

If you liked this book, me, and my nonsense, you can join my reader's group **Amy's Sinful Sweethearts.**

They always get first dibs on ARCs, signed copies, and giveaways.

If you like my writing, take a look at my backlist. I have some goodies there.

Hope to see you soon xx